LONG RIDE TO YUMA

Clyde Manson, a high-flyer from New York, rides from the Mexican border to Sasabe, Arizona, to rob the bank. Riding with him is Hoss Kemp and the Mexican, Guerrero. However, Manson has his own agenda . . . When they rob the bank, they leave Deputy Marshal Will Hawker shot dead, and escape across the arid Arizona deserts, chased by Marshal Slade Hawker and his posse. And during the final, bloody showdown, Deputy US Marshal Wyatt Earp makes his sinister presence felt.

WILL KEEN

LONG RIDE TO YUMA

Complete and Unabridged

LINFORD
Leicester

First published in Great Britain in 2009 by
Robert Hale Limited
London

First Linford Edition
published 2010
by arrangement with
Robert Hale Limited
London

British Library CIP Data

Keen, Will, *1936* –
  Long ride to Yuma. - -
  (Linford western library)
  1. Bank robberies- -Arizona- -Fiction.
  2. Western stories. 3. Large type books.
  I. Title
  823.9'2–dc22

ISBN 978–1–44480–473–7

Published by
F. A. Thorpe (Publishing)
Anstey, Leicestershire

Set by Words & Graphics Ltd.
Anstey, Leicestershire
Printed and bound in Great Britain by
T. J. International Ltd., Padstow, Cornwall

This book is printed on acid-free paper

PART ONE

THE POSSE

Prologue

They camped under thirty-foot high saguaro cactuses bordering a dry wash to the west of Nogales, the clatter of the three horses disturbing several Gila woodpeckers as they rode in. The sun was a blood-red disc over the mountains to the far west of Sonora. By the time the men had built a fire, cooked supper and brewed a pot of strong coffee, the sun was down and the mountains had been reduced to a vague purple haze stretching like a shadow across the horizon. The border between Arizona Territory and Mexico, less than a mile to the south of their position, was an imaginary line; their boundary, their world, was the circle of flickering light cast by the crackling fire.

'Forty miles,' Guerrero said. 'Three, maybe four hours' riding to Sasabe. *Es fácil.*'

'Set off at dawn, we're there when the town blinks, yawns and comes awake,' Clyde Manson said. 'Awake, but not alert.'

Manson was not the kind of man normally to be found in a rough camp on the Mexican border. He was tall and elegant, his speech was educated and carried the accents and cadences of the East, his range clothes looked too new and the blue eyes studying his companions were more than ordinarily intelligent. A shrewd observer might have taken one look and guessed that Manson was a businessman from somewhere like New York, or Philadelphia, fallen on hard times, and he would have been right. But that description would merely have been scratching the surface of a complex man who had chosen, because of a series of misadventures, to embark on undertakings that not only put his life in danger, but were operating a long way outside the law.

'*Es fácil.*'

The third man, Hoss Kemp, was echoing the Mexican's words. All three men laughed, the fire gleaming on white teeth and dancing on the cold blued metal of the pistols at their belts, the Winchester rifles lying alongside blanket rolls and saddles.

'Easy, yes,' Manson said, 'because we're hitting a small town. In and out. Then another. Ajo. Then Gila Bend. Mohawk, maybe — unless by then or before then we've got enough so that we can call it a day and push on all the way.'

'To Yuma,' Guerrero said, nodding sagely. 'And when we get to Yuma with this enough that by then will be bulging our saddle-bags — then what?'

'Then it's Ben,' Manson said. 'My brother, Ben, and the end of a long hard road to justice.'

'You transmitted the wire?'

'From Nogales, to Yuma? Yes. To a certain prison warden who's now rubbing his fat hands as he looks out of his office window. Watching, with impatience and greed, for three riders with fat saddle-bags.' He grinned. 'You were there, Guerrero. You saw me write it with a stub of pencil, saw the telegraph man check it, pass it as OK — '

'I speak English very well but — '

'Very well,' Kemp said, eyebrows raised, and he and Manson grinned without rancour at the Mexican.

'But my reading is not so very well,' Guerrero went on as he matched their broad grins. 'So now I am making sure, before we proceed, what I see with my eyes is what happens, *exactamente, sin lugar a dudas*, which is to say — '

'Yes, yes, I got it right, no question, amigo,' Manson said, nodding. 'That's the way it is. *Exactamente.*'

'So after the business with the wire, and a succession of small towns that take us eventually to the *ciudad* of Yuma with its *prisión* and your brother — after that . . . ?'

'After that,' Hoss Kemp said, 'you and me, we're in the dark.'

6

For the first time there was a faint hint of annoyance in his voice as he looked at Manson.

'We know how some of the cash we accumulate in a succession of highly risky ventures will be used, but what happens to the rest of it? You about to enlighten us, Manson?'

'Cash has a habit of dribbling through a man's fingers. I want it to grow, for us, for you, me, for Ben — for all of us. I've got it all figured out, trust me — '

'Manson is a *caballero*.' Guerrero said, as if talking to himself, and now his white teeth glistened beneath his fine moustache, but the grin failed to reach his liquid black eyes. 'He is a *caballero*, but like us he is also a *bandido* — and yet he is asking us to a *confiar en él*, to trust him — '

'You've got no choice,' Manson said bluntly.

'But yes, we have *every* choice.'

'Leave it, Guerrero,' Kemp said impatiently, and he stabbed a finger at

Manson. 'Sasabe. Why there first? Why not another small town? One closer to Yuma would make more sense, save riding halfway across Arizona Territory with stolen banknotes busting from our saddle-bags.'

'There's a man in Sasabe with a debt to pay,' Manson said, and as the sudden edge in his voice made the other two men exchange swift glances, understanding flared in Kemp's eyes.

'This debt got anything to do with your brother?'

'Not *anything*,' Manson corrected, '*everything*.'

'And this man,' Guerrero said, 'he is aware that you are about to collect?'

'He's not aware now,' Manson said, 'and when he does realize what's happening he'll be looking into the muzzle of my six-gun and bracing himself for the bullet that will end his miserable life.'

★ ★ ★

The next day, in a low timber office block on a naked ridge overlooking the lights of Tombstone, Arizona, another three men were sitting at a long table. Blinds were pulled down over the small windows. A single oil lamp with a battered tin reflector cast its light over just a small portion of that room. Beneath it, the smoke from expensive cigars swirled and eddied. The men were all dressed in dark suits. String ties were pulled down from white collars loosened around glistening, fleshy necks.

Instead of coffee from tin cups, the men were drinking expensive whiskey from crystal glasses. The heavy glasses did not belong to them. They and the whiskey they contained were the property of the man who should have been sitting at the head of the table. Some three months previously, in July of 1880, he had been shot dead by a drunken cowboy as he walked out of the Eagle Brewery on the corner of Fifth and Allen Streets.

When Frank 'Haggerty' Hainsworth

dropped dead in a pool of blood, his big heart ripped asunder by the blast from a powerful six-gun, the Silver Lode Mining Company that was his brain child was effectively finished. He was the man with the drive, the personality, the intimate knowledge of silver mining. He was also the man with the money. Regularly over the past three months the men who were his business colleagues had gathered around the table agonizing over how to keep going while all around them vital supplies were dwindling, hard-working men were clamouring for wages and the banks were turning stony faces to entreaties that lacked the weight of collateral.

This latest, late-night meeting had been called out of desperation. At least one of the men had been recommending that they cut and run. That man was Dane Swift. Now, ten minutes after the door had banged shut, match flames had been applied to fat cigars and whiskey splashed into the late Frank Hainsworth's sparkling glasses, the man who had been planning a new life in California was sitting back in his chair and looking smug.

'Swallowed the cream,' Dougie Grant said, rocking as he watched Swift.

'Aye, and then the cat got his tongue.'

That was Ernest Gallagher, the bruiser of the trio, the Scotsman who spent a lot of time getting his hands dirty alongside the men mining the silver. He had no time for banks, but knew that without money no project could succeed. He left the negotiating to the other two men, but was fast running out of patience.

'So what is it?' he said now. 'Have you a light in your eye because your passage is booked? Are you letting us know that you're away from Tombstone on the morrow?'

'Not tomorrow,' Swift said. 'There's no longer any need to run like dogs with our tails between our legs. When we do walk out of here we'll walk out with our heads high and money in the bank.'

11

'The banks don't want to know you,' Gallagher said bluntly, 'and if you've got any money to put in there it'll be swallowed up.'

'New money,' Swift said.

'New money from where?'

Swift met Grant's challenging gaze.

'I've been doing some quiet negotiating. To keep the banks in the dark and ensure secrecy I needed to hide everything from you. Now that the deal's done, I can apologize. And, yes, the deal is done. As you know, I was in Benson yesterday. A final offer came in by telegraph, and it's an offer we cannot refuse — '

'Be very careful,' Grant said, again cutting in. 'Bank drafts, cheques, they can all go belly up. If those bank drafts come from an unreliable source . . . '

He pulled a face, glanced across at Gallagher who simply shrugged.

'This is cash,' Swift said quietly, and there was quiet amusement in his eyes as he watched his companions digest the startling news.

'A time of seven days was mooted,' Swift went on. 'I agreed. When that time or its approximation has elapsed, a man will walk in here and on this table he will spread enough cash to buy us out.' He grinned at Gallagher. 'California's still there in my sights, Paddy, only the dream's become a reality.'

'Has he got a name?' Grant said, 'this mysterious benefactor?'

'He's intelligent, and a humorist,' Swift said. 'He calls himself Midas.'

1

It was well past midnight when eighteen-year-old Nathan Creed walked unsteadily out of the Buenos Tiempos saloon in Sasabe, Arizona. He wore tipped back on his head the battered, flat-crowned black hat with silver conchos sewn on its band that he had picked up on a trip into Mexico. He walked carefully, but the worn-down heels of his boots rolled on the rough plank walk. He staggered, muttered a soft, 'Whoa, there,' as he listed gently to one side and, with intense concentration, rested his weight carefully against one of the mesquite poles supporting the ramada. There, his shoulder occasionally slipping off old peeled wood worn slick by the grasp of countless hands — and drawing a startled 'Whoops' from parted lips — he dug out the makings and began rolling a cigarette.

He did it well, chuckling throatily as he managed to get most of the tobacco flakes into the paper, the paper rolled into a misshapen cylinder. He stuck the somewhat flattened cylinder between his lips. It hung there, quivering and shedding tobacco as he twisted his lips this way and that way in a grimace and patted his pockets for a Lucifer. He tried to focus his gaze on the cigarette between his lips, and succeeded only in crossing his eyes. Then, wagging his head in drunken appreciation of his quick thinking, he took the cigarette out of his mouth and cupped it in his hand to avoid further damage.

Suddenly, with his other hand trapped in his pocket, he grunted in shock as a tremendous blow struck him between the shoulders. He hit the mesquite pole with his head, lost his footing and fell sprawling on the warm boards. Prostrate, head ringing, he heard two men roaring with laughter as they fled, their pounding boots vibrating the boards beneath his face.

'Sons of bitches.'

Cursing softly and with a noticeable slurring of the sibilants, he clambered to his feet. He opened his fist, stared blankly at the crumpled ruins of his cigarette, then threw it high in the air and tilted his head backwards to watch the shreds of paper and tobacco float away on the breeze. The move was his undoing. He promptly spun dizzily and fell off the plank walk into the street.

It was a drop of two-and-a-half feet. He hit hard, and rolled under the hitch rail. That put him too close to the stamping, razor-sharp hoofs of his skittish pony. He rose, spitting dust, grabbed a stirrup and hauled himself upright. Then, breathing hard and rubbing his ribs, he climbed aboard the brown-and-white pinto, looped the reins in his palm and leaned forward with both hands resting on the saddle horn.

'All right then,' he said harshly, 'if that's the way you want it.' And as he looked down the street, there was menace in his voice, and a vindictiveness out of all proportion with the rough but harmless prank that had been played on him.

The two men who had slammed into him were clear in the moonlight. As Creed watched, they split up. One crossed the street, heading for the livery barn. The other, the taller and broader of the two, turned into the jail.

Creed grinned lopsidedly. Sasabe was a border settlement in the Altar Valley — not big enough to call a town, in Creed's opinion. There was a saloon — Good Times, if you wanted it in English — a general store, a livery barn at the end of the one wide, dusty street, with a big corral out back. A bank, too, which Creed's pa managed; the main office was in Phoenix. And a jail. With an honest to goodness marshal, and his ornery brother who was also deputy marshal: Slade and Will Hawker.

The marshal and his jail were special for two reasons. First was that a settlement the size of Sasabe wouldn't have a lawman of any kind if it wasn't for the proximity of the border with Mexico. The second was that the adobe building housing the jail and the office was the only business premises in Sasabe that didn't bear Nathan Creed's very special signature.

That was about to be rectified.

With a click of his tongue and a flick of the reins, Creed started his horse down the street. It was less than fifty yards to the jail. There was nobody about. By the time he'd covered half the distance he had a Colt .44 in each hand and was guiding the paint with his knees.

The man who had entered the jail had slammed the door behind him; the thud of its closing had drifted up the street to Creed. The office windows — one either side of the door — were small and barred. Creed could see the light glowing inside the room. Shadows drifted between the light and the windows. As he drew closer he could hear the murmur of voices.

Then he was level with the building. With a nudge of his right knee he turned the pinto. Then he settled himself in the saddle, and opened fire.

He had six shells in each Colt. Adobe chips flew from holes punched in the walls as he planted a neat row of six spaced shots beneath each window. He took his time. Gunsmoke coiled around his head as the six-guns kicked in his hands. Muzzle flashes lit up the white walls. The fierce crackle of the explosions bounced back from the adobe and was absorbed by the night.

Then the door crashed open.

Two men piled out, bare-headed. Guns glittered in their fists. On their chests, badges in the shape of stars glinted in the moonlight.

With a mighty 'Yee-hah', Creed spun both pistols so that they entered their respective holsters with a dull thunk, wheeled his horse away from the squat building and raked it with his spurs. Flattened along the pony's neck, arms outstretched above its head so that the reins were held high and the horse's soft mane flared in his face, he pulled a long plume of dust behind him as he left town at a furious gallop with the loud yells of angry men and his own helpless laughter ringing in his ears.

* * *

He'd expected the house to be in darkness when he arrived home, but, as he rode around to the small corral and settled the pinto in the stable for the night, he was aware that the oil lamp was still lit in the main room. He lingered, knowing that more trouble was brewing. When he finally left the corral, made his way back along the white picket fence and walked up the path to the steps, his father's tall, bearded figure was a menacing shape in the doorway.

'We live too damn close to town for your good,' Alexander Creed said. 'I could hear the shooting and the shouting even before I heard you hammering that pony down the trail.'

'Nothing more to say, then,' Nathan Creed said, and he stepped up and tried to push his way in.

'You think not?' his father said, his bulk blocking the way. 'I'm beginning to believe it's wrong for you to live at home. You cause so much trouble you'd be better off out of here; better off in a room at that drinking den where you perform menial tasks, on your own where the only harm you do is to yourself.'

'Strikes me that's what you've been planning for some time,' his son said bitterly. 'First Ma, now me — '

Alexander Creed didn't answer. Instead, he stepped back a pace, cocked his big fist and stopped Nathan's angry retort with a mighty blow hammered to the face. Nathan Creed reeled backwards. His foot turned on the edge of the step. One hand clamped to the blood gushing from his nose, he toppled sideways. He crumpled to break his fall, hit hard-packed earth and smashed into the shrubbery. A broken branch ripped the soft skin of his neck. Flat on his back, he looked up at the doorway, automatically lifting a crooked arm to ward off the inevitable kick. It didn't come; the doorway was empty. He sucked in a wet breath, spat a red spray into the grass as he rolled onto his belly and got his knees under him. As he climbed to his feet and replaced his hat he heard the drum of hoofs and closed his watering eyes in despair. When he opened them again, Deputy Will Hawker was swinging down from his horse and big Alexander Creed was back in the doorway with his hands planted on his hips.

Hawker came up the path with his hand on his six-gun. Sharp grey eyes swiftly took in Nathan Creed's bloody face, the looming figure of Alexander Creed with fists on hips. The deputy shook his head.

'He don't understand that treatment, Creed. His kind never do.'

'My ma does,' Nathan said thickly.

'That's why she up and walked out on him. Though why the hell she's taken up with your brother's beyond my understanding.'

Hawker ignored him. 'This time he shot up the jail,' he said, looking at Alexander Creed. 'I can take him in for that, let him stew a couple of weeks in a cell while he ponders the meaning of his miserable life. However, I respect your position as manager of the bank and if you can give your word — '

'Forget that,' Creed said. 'Throw him in jail, for a night, for a week, who the hell cares. Just get him out of my sight.'

He turned on his heel and stalked inside. The door slammed, shuddering in its frame.

Hawker grinned at Nathan.

'I'll wait here while you get your horse.'

★ ★ ★

Marshal Slade Hawker was as tall as his younger brother, but he carried his bulk

24

as lightly as a dancer while giving the impression of a steel spring ready to uncoil at lightning speed. Even seated he exuded an air of dangerous efficiency, and he was behind his desk clearing up for the night when Will Hawker ushered the blood-smeared Nathan Creed inside.

A frown shadowed the marshal's face as he looked at the young man's battered countenance.

'Don't look at me,' Will said easily. 'He'd arrived home when I caught up, so one shrewd guess'll tell you who altered the kid's appearance.'

'What's he here for?'

'Paying for his sins.'

'Looks like that's been taken care of by his pa. A few bullet holes don't make much difference to the look of this place, but giving him room and board in a cell means the good folk of the town are paying his keep.'

'Alexander kicked him out.'

Slade sat back, nodding thoughtfully. Absently fingering the badge pinned to

25

his vest, he seemed to be weighing up options, none of which was pleasing.

'You're welcome to stay at my place, kid,' he said at last. 'There's a spare room, and your ma would be delighted to have you close to her.' He shrugged. 'Here or at my place, it's your call.'

'Close to her means close to you. What does that give me? I swap a tinpot tyrant for a hard man who rode in from Tombstone a couple of months ago and swept my ma off her feet. You call that a choice?'

Nathan Creed's words were muffled as he used his bandanna to mop at the trickle of blood still leaking from his nose. Like Slade Hawker, he was looking at what was on offer and not liking the view.

'When he wasn't smashing me in the face, Pa was suggesting a room at the saloon would suit me. If I'm not being charged . . . '

But Hawker was on his feet, shaking his head as he took a bunch of keys down from a wall peg.

'That wasn't on offer. Will's right, a night in a cell will maybe show you the error of your ways. If your nose needs fixing, I'll call Doc Kennedy. It's too late for supper, but there's coffee if you want it. Otherwise that's it until breakfast.'

Still talking, he was already making his way through to the cells, keys jingling. Nathan Creed stumbled as Deputy Will Hawker pushed him hard between the shoulder blades. That made it twice in one night, Creed thought. Tight-lipped, recalling the earlier incident that had tipped him over the edge, he followed the tall marshal through to the gloom deep inside the building.

★ ★ ★

Battered and bloody, his head a throbbing ache from the strong poison he had poured into his system while in the Buenos Tiempos, Nathan Creed sat on the corn husk mattress with his knees drawn up to his chin, his arms wrapped around his shins. The sound of the cell door clanging shut was still echoing mockingly in his ears. The light from the oil lamp hanging in the area between facing cells revealed the awful emptiness of the room he inhabited; the emptiness in his soul was indescribable, and almost too much for him to bear.

Yet from the depths of his misery, Nathan Creed was drawing inspiration. A man, he figured, could get only so low before he was forced to climb back up, or perish. Besides, hadn't he seen this day coming?

He had begun his working life as a promising young bronc buster, but a badly broken left arm and subsequent attempts to continue riding had shown him that, at seventeen, he was finished.

From then on life had gone rapidly downhill. His father's offer of a job in the bank and training at head office in Phoenix had been turned down, and by a circuitous route Nathan still couldn't fathom he'd ended up as a swamper in the Buenos Tiempos.

That fine establishment had quickly

become his second home, a situation hastened by Alexander Creed's worsening treatment of his wife, and of his son at those rare times when he did return to the family home.

But 'family home' was a misnomer. Nathan Creed had watched his mother, religious and ever faithful to her marriage vows, wither and fade under the relentless domination of her wealthy husband in a house that had become a virtual prison. That situation, Nathan knew, would have continued indefinitely had it not been for the arrival in Sasabe of a young lawman.

Slade Hawker had worked in Tombstone as deputy marshal under city marshal Virgil Earp. When a prominent, unarmed businessman had been shot dead late one night outside the Eagle Brewery, Hawker had arrested the killer and brought him to justice. But the man's angry relatives had made things so hot for Hawker that, on the advice of Cochise County Sheriff John Behan, the young deputy had left town.

He had ended up in Sasabe, and within a short time been joined by his brother who had been drifting north along the Rio Bravo.

Creed stirred, wincing as he straightened his legs, then grimacing as the act of wincing sent a stab of pain through his damaged nose. He shook his head angrily — then discovered that simply added to the pain, and threw back his head to laugh out loud.

Better. He swung his legs off the cot and stood up. The high barred window let in the cool night air. He could smell mesquite and sage and horses, the dust of the street, the warm stink of the coal oil burning in Sasabe's street lamps.

But as well as those smells, as Nathan Creed paced the small cell he could also smell the wind of change. That change had been inevitable from the moment when, one week after he had walked into the job of town marshal, Slade Hawker stole Mollie Creed from under husband Alexander's nose and moved her into his cabin on the outskirts of town.

If that had been a defining moment for his ma, Nathan thought, delighting in the clarity of thought that for so long had eluded him, then his defining moment had come less than an hour ago when Alexander had driven his fist into his face and knocked him flat in the shrubbery.

Enough was enough, Nathan thought. One way or another it was time to pick himself up and move on. How he would do that, and the direction he would take, were unclear. But as he returned to the hard cot and flopped down for the night, he knew without any doubt whatsoever that while tomorrow was always another day, his tomorrow was going to be the most momentous day of his young life.

He wasn't to know it, but even as he fell into a doze, then a deep and satisfying sleep, the men who were to change his life forever were already thundering along the trail towards Sasabe.

2

To Deputy Will Hawker, stretching his legs on the plank walk outside the jail, the three horsemen riding into Sasabe from the south-east appeared as shimmering black shapes delineated by the dazzling orb of the still rising sun. To watch their approach he was forced to shade his eyes with his hand. Even then, the shapes lacked detail — yet without detail of any kind, they were still a cause for concern.

Three men, Will mused, turning his back to the sun's brilliance as black blotches danced before his eyes. The locals he knew who lived in outlying areas would not arrive in town in threes, and few would arrive at this time of day. Strangers tended to ride on by, rarely noticing the sleepy, sun-soaked Arizona town. So this was an unusual occurrence — and, as Will snatched a final, squint-eyed glance up the street, he saw that the three men had drawn rein in front of the bank.

The door swung behind him as he entered the office. Slade Hawker was at the stove, pouring coffee. There was a question in his eyes as he looked at his brother, noted the tenseness in his demeanour.

'Strangers,' Will said. 'They've stopped at the bank.'

'That's where folk keep their cash,' Slade said. 'If they need it, that's where they go.'

'When's the last time you saw three riders at the bank this time of day?'

Slade turned from the stove, a steaming tin cup in his hand. There was a tin plate on the desk containing fried beef, two fried eggs with glistening yellow yolks. He picked up the plate and, with both hands full, turned and headed for the inner door.

'I'd look into it, but the kid's demanding his breakfast,' he said over his shoulder. 'Those men worry you, take a walk up the street.'

'I might just do that,' Will said, and he crossed the office and took a shotgun from the rack.

* * *

Clyde Manson slipped the Winchester out of the boot under his right leg and rested the gleaming weapon across his thighs. Kemp and Guerrero had already swung down. They handed their horses' reins to Manson, and he looped them loosely around his saddle horn.

The bank was not yet open. As the stocky Mexican and the lean Texan with the pale eyes moved towards the building, their bodies were taut with impatience. Gloved hands rested on the butts of six-guns. Boots scuffed dust as the men paused in their walk and turned this way and that, warily studying the street for curious onlookers, for men whose cut suggested they might pose a danger. Nothing. The street was empty of life.

Outside the gunsmith's a big wooden

34

sign creaked on rusting iron brackets. Manson thought he saw a man watching from an upstairs window. Kemp started visibly as a tumbleweed rolled in the warm breeze, rasping against the plank walk.

Guerrero laughed softly at his companion's disquiet, and muttered something under his breath in Spanish.

Behind them, like a heavy plank falling in the stillness, the bank's doors banged open.

Startled, Manson's big roan moved sharply. It nudged the other horses as it backed, swinging its rear end, its tail twitching.

'We're being watched,' Manson said, gazing down the street.

'From that window across the street, and from the jail, I think,' Guerrero said. 'The sun at our backs is helpful. It tells me for sure that building is the jail, for its windows have bars, and that man, he is wearing a badge.'

'Now isn't that dandy?' Manson said softly.

'Damn it, no, it's just what we don't

want,' Kemp said curtly. 'Manson, you make damn sure you keep your eyes on that fellow.'

'Since when have you been giving the orders?'

'Since you figured it was easier to sit out here and let us do your dirty work for you.'

'Believe me, there's a good reason for playing it this way,' Manson said easily, and he grinned and raised his eyebrows. 'Well? What the hell are you two waiting for? You expect that cash to come leaping out at you?'

Guerrero spat in the dust.

'Do as Kemp tells you and watch that lawman,' he said harshly, 'or, who knows, perhaps the plenty money for that brother of yours — '

'Shut your damn mouth and get on with it,' Manson growled, and for an instant the Winchester's muzzle swung to cover the Mexican.

He watched as a simmering Guerrero returned to dig a gunny sack from his saddle-bag. That done both men hesitated, then drew their six-guns and held them down by their thighs. Then, after a quick exchange of glances, they walked up the steps and into the bank.

No going back now, Manson thought, feeling a grotesque grin tightening his face, the sweat coating his hands inside skin-tight gloves. This was it, the beginning, the first of several such raids which would stretch like stepping stones across Arizona territory, forming a precarious pathway to one young man's freedom. And, Manson thought with a surge of emotion, to his own return to the world of business where once again he would take his place at the pinnacle, a man of substance, always respected, always looked up to.

Only half listening, he heard Kemp roaring fierce commands which would cause terrified bank staff to freeze. Manson returned his gaze to the street. His pulse quickened. The man wearing the badge, the Sasabe marshal, had now moved away from the jail and was heading towards the bank. He was tall, just the way Ben had described the lawman, Slade Hawker, who had arrested him on that night in Tombstone.

Easy now, Manson thought, mentally reaching out to the advancing lawman. *Not too damn fast, you take your time, fellow. Get here when Kemp and Guerrero come piling out carrying stolen money. Then you'll have an excuse for going for your gun, and that'll give me a damn good reason for dropping you in your tracks — as if I haven't got a good enough reason already.*

Even as those thoughts raced through his brain he saw that the approaching lawman had quickened his pace. He'd weighed up the situation, had seen two men enter the bank and had realized that the one man left outside was holding all three horses. The classic set up for a bank raid — he can't mistake it, Manson thought with satisfaction, because that was the way it had been planned.

Carefully, without making the movement obvious, he worked the Winchester's lever and a bullet was rammed into the rifle's breech with an oily click. But the loud voices in the bank had faded into silence, the town was too quiet, the sound from the Winchester too loud. With a sharp intake of breath Manson saw the lawman's head jerk up — and suddenly he became aware that the tall man was carrying a shotgun.

Manson cursed softly. His horse sensed something was wrong. The big roan was becoming difficult to hold. Easier to walk him a few paces, up the street and back, settle him — but holding the other horses ruled that out.

Another glance down the street. The lawman was closing fast.

Twisting in the saddle, Manson looked towards the bank. In the shadows beyond the open door, he detected movement. But now all three horses were restless. The roan snorted. Guerrero's buckskin reared half-heartedly, ears pricked. Kemp's mare backed away, straining. Becoming desperate, Manson looped the reins more tightly round the horn and lifted the Winchester.

'Kemp,' he cried.

'Yeah,' came the answering yell, and suddenly the two men tumbled from the bank, falling over each other in their haste, six-guns flashing in the bright sunlight.

Down the street, dust spurted as the lawman broke into a run. He called out, his words lost as the three outlaws came together in a rush.

'Mount up,' Manson said to Kemp and Guerrero, letting their mounts' reins slip loose. 'Get the hell out of here, leave him to me.'

'Ah yes,' Guerrero said, laughing breathlessly as he threw himself onto his buckskin, the heavy sack swinging. 'This is the man who is about to repay a debt — '

'And put us in deep trouble,' Kemp said.

Already mounted, he swung his horse, glared across at Manson.

'Leave him be. Bank robbery's bad

enough without adding murder.'

He spun away, spurred his horse at an angle across the street then turned to ride hard into the rising sun. Guerrero went after him, big sombrero slipping down his back to hang flapping by its throat cord.

The lawman was thirty yards away from the bank.

'Hawker,' Manson called. 'Is your name Hawker?'

'Never mind my name, put down your gun and — '

'I need to know your name. I'm looking for a man named Hawker. Is that you?'

'Yes, I'm Hawker, now do as I say and drop that gun.'

Manson shook his head, tightened his thighs on the roan, held it steady. He rammed the Winchester's butt into his shoulder. Across the sights he saw the lawman, Hawker, register his move. The tall man was caught in the open. He looked left, right, knew Sasabe's wide main street left him with nowhere to go.

He dropped to one knee. Manson followed the movement with the Winchester's barrel, letting it fall, the front sight always lined up on the lawman's chest.

He knew it made no difference, yet something deep inside him told him to wait. He watched, rocking gently to the roan's movement, easily holding his aim. He let the lawman get the shotgun to his shoulder; let him ease his finger onto the trigger; let him begin that last, fateful squeeze — swore, later, that from a distance of thirty yards he could see the tall man's knuckle whiten with the pressure.

Clyde Manson pulled the trigger.

In self defence — if anyone was interested.

He saw the lawman rock with the impact. Saw dark blood blossom instantly on his shirt front, shining wetly. Then the tall man went down. Already on one knee, he simply toppled sideways and lay motionless in the dust.

And as another tall man emerged

from the jail and began running up the street, a badge glittering on his vest, Clyde Manson smoothly pouched his Winchester then swung the roan and rode out of town.

3

Nathan Creed was still eating his breakfast when the shot rang out — though rang out wasn't quite right, he thought, fork poised over the greasy plate. More of a crack softened by distance, he corrected, then tilted his head as he tried to figure out the source of the gunfire, and what was going on.

The angle of the sun slanting through the barred window told him it was still very early morning. The shot had been fired from a rifle. The shootist was some way away, but definitely in town.

Even as he was making that judgement he heard the rapid beat of hooves receding in the distance. Then the office door banged open and feet pounded on the plank walk. At the same time he heard shouting, more rapid footsteps, all moving in the same direction. Up town.

And then Nathan was down off the bed, breakfast forgotten as he realized that the one building of note that lay in that direction was the bank managed by his father. He ran to the bars, grabbed them, twisted his neck and flattened his cheek against them as he tried in vain to see into the office through the closed door.

'Slade,' he roared. 'Let me out of here.'

Then common sense took over. Running feet meant Slade Hawker had gone to sort out the trouble. His brother, Deputy Will Hawker, had left the office a little earlier with his night shift finished. Will was a tough fellow. If he needed Slade's help, something was badly wrong.

For the next thirty minutes, Nathan fretted with impatience as he tried to piece together the unfolding story from the multitude of sounds coming to his ears. Fingering his bruised and battered face, he paced the cell. Once he tried to reach the barred window and peer out, but found it way out of his reach. That brought a strong and violent reaction: angrily he flung his empty plate at the bars imprisoning him and, fists on hips, watched it roll across the dirt floor.

Then the door leading to the office opened. Slade Hawker strode through, his face drawn and bleak. Keys jangled as he opened the cell door and waved Nathan out.

'You're free to go.'

'I heard a shot. What happened?'

'The bank was robbed. Your father's unhurt, but angry.'

'Where's Will?'

Hawker took a deep breath.

'My brother's dead. I'm about to raise a posse, so I want you out of here now — '

'I'll go with you. Swear me in — '

'No.'

'I can shoot.' Nathan waved a hand. 'But you know that, most of the businesses in town can swear — '

'Goddamn it, Nathan, you think this is a joke? Come on, out of here, let me get on with my job.'

Hawker swung on his heel. As Nathan followed him into the office he could hear excited voices out in the street, the stamp of many feet on the plank walks. Hawker walked out, leaving the street door open. As Nathan slapped on his black hat and stepped out into the hot sunlight he saw a buckboard slowly heading down town transporting a blanket-covered shape. Several men on horseback were gathered in the street outside the jail. Watched by men and women shaded by the galleries they moved their horses closer and began listening intently to Slade Hawker.

'This morning, three men rode into town,' Hawker said, his voice flat. 'They robbed the bank, taking several thousand dollars of your hard-earned money. One of them murdered Deputy Will Hawker. Will was my brother, but' — he paused, waited as voices were raised angrily, then went on — 'but pursuing those men is a matter for the law. I'm after volunteers. The men who ride with me will be sworn in as deputies.'

Again he waited. There was a subdued muttering from the gathered men. Then, one by one, hands were raised. It was clear from that spontaneous reaction that not a single man wished to be left behind. Hawker looked them over critically, then stepped down into the street. He spoke to each man in turn, holding bridles, looking up into hard, anxious faces as he spoke. Nathan saw him shake his head several times, and knew that many of the volunteers were unsuitable: too old; too young; family men with too much to lose; others who were fit and strong but carried pistols clumsily, rusty from lack of use.

At the finish, just three men remained.

With reluctance, Hawker thanked the others, dismissed them and watched them ride away. Then he took the three successful volunteers into the office and in a soft voice swore them in as deputies.

'We leave in one hour,' he told them.

'Go home, say what has to be said and get what you need — jerky, water, blanket rolls. A rifle, ammunition. And men — from the bottom of my heart, I thank you.'

★ ★ ★

'Three's not enough,' Nathan Creed said.

'I thought I told you to get out of here.'

'That was a mistake. You're off chasing bank robbers, outlaws. They're also killers, so you need good men.'

'Good men?' Hawker managed a smile. 'You're a swamper, Nathan. You work in the Buenos Tiempos. In case you've forgotten, that's a saloon. You earn a few bucks washing floors, and use them daily to get roostered. When that's done, you destroy property.'

'Step outside,' Nathan said, 'and look at the line of shots I placed under your windows. The men you've deputized couldn't do that stone cold sober.'

'You've got one thing right,' Hawker said. 'You have it in you to be good. What you need is direction.'

He was busy as he talked. Most of the time his back was turned to Creed as he dug boxes of cartridges out of desk drawers, selected a rifle from the gun rack, searched the office for his canteen.

'Direction?' Creed said cautiously.

'Charlie Birrel over at the gunsmith's is looking for someone to learn the trade. Should suit you, Nathan . . . '

The big lawman's words trailed off as he banged a gleaming Winchester and tin canteen on the desk and began hunting for coffee and supplies to take with him on what could prove to be a long, hard chase. Nathan Creed watched him absently for a couple more minutes. Then he walked out into the morning heat and, after a moment's hesitation, set off towards Charlie Birrel's shop.

So far, he thought ruefully, although a lot had happened that was both unusual and life-changing for certain people in Sasabe, nothing much had happened to make his day momentous. Charlie Birrel ran a successful business in a land where success for a skilful man working with guns wasn't all that difficult to achieve. But was that kind of work, Nathan wondered, the dramatic change he was looking for? Or — and this was a sudden thought that sent excitement coursing through his veins — had Marshal Hawker, by pointing him in the gunsmith's direction, unwittingly shown him the open door to unforeseen opportunities?

Nathan quickened his pace.

The town had quietened after the early morning excitement, and was back to its searing, midsummer somnolence. Nathan met nobody as he tramped across the wide, dusty street, and when he pushed his way into Birrel's shop it was cool, empty, and smelling most enticingly of clean gun oil.

Birrel was behind the counter, pen in hand, glasses perched on the end of his hooked nose. He looked up. Brilliant blue eyes set in a face like old leather capped by cropped grey hair settled on Nathan's damaged features.

'What happened, kid, you had an altercation with a fractious door?'

'Yeah, very funny, Charlie. Happens there's a lot been going on in town.'

'From what I've seen, none of it concerns you.'

'In a roundabout way, it does.'

'That means you'd like it to, but you ain't got there yet,' Birrel said, and then he grinned. 'Why aren't you washing floors, Nathan?'

'I just told you, too much going on. The bank's been robbed, Will Hawker's dead.'

The amusement was wiped from Birrel's face as he nodded.

'I was upstairs, and saw it all. Heard the shouting, the shots, saw Will go down.' He shook his head gravely. 'Saw Slade arrive on the scene. He must be going crazy.'

'I guess. It took him a while, but in

the end he raised a three-man posse.'

That caused a raised eyebrow.

'When do you leave?'

'I, er, don't. They leave in an hour, but Slade doesn't want me along.'

'You shoot better drunk than most men do sober,' Birrel said, echoing Nathan's words.

'You should know. You taught me everything, over my pa's objections. Took me out back on that waste ground. Taught me to squeeze not pull a trigger, to make every shot count — '

'But I didn't expect you to use what I taught you and shoot up the town most Saturday nights.'

'More often that,' Creed said, somewhat shamefaced. 'Wrong, yes, but better to drill holes in a few false fronts than something more serious — like getting into gunfights, maybe ending up killing a man.'

Birrel nodded slowly.

'So if you're not riding with the posse,' he said, 'who's the three?'

'Morg Stanley, Wes Costigan, Arn Mills.'

'Jesus Christ,' Charlie Birrel said, and he straightened for the first time and flung his glasses on the counter. 'There's not a man there under fifty. Has Slade gone plumb crazy.'

Nathan shrugged. 'Best he could do. You should see the ones he turned down.'

Birrel came around the counter, crossed to the window and looked out at the sun beating down on the dust of the town. He was middling in height, but broad-shouldered, straight as a pole and bursting with good health. Nathan had watched him at target practice, and knew he could punch the centre out of the ace of spades at thirty yards with his Colt .45 Peacemaker. With his '73 Winchester repeating rifle he invariably took top prize at the Pima County fair, and if that didn't make him good enough . . .

'What that man and his posse of old-timers need,' Birrel was saying softly, 'is a couple of good men watching their backs. Does that make sense to you?'

'Best sense I've heard all day.'

Birrel swung to face Nathan Creed.

'Well, you said in a roundabout way this concerns you, so I take it that means you're with me, young feller?'

'All the way,' Nathan said, grinning. 'Put one of those fancy rifles in my hands' — this said while nodding at the polished racks beyond the counter — 'and you and me'll be primed to finish off the bandits when those old fellers in the posse fall by the wayside.'

4

Beyond an arid ridge topped by parched trees that hid them from the town of Sasabe, Clyde Manson lifted a hand and the three bank robbers wheeled their horses and changed their course from east to north-west. Immediately, and again at Manson's command, they slowed their frantic pace. The contours of the land meant that comparatively high ground remained between them and the town. With no reason to believe pursuit would be heading in their direction, they were able to ease the lathered horses then pull them to a halt in the meagre shade until their breath stopped rasping, the heaving of the glistening flanks under their thighs had subsided.

'Is one hundred miles to Ajo,' Guerrero said, puffing on a black cheroot as he plucked restlessly at the cord of his sombrero. 'After that, is another thirty or forty to Gila Bend, heading north. *Dirección equivocada*, you understand me? Wrong way? If you go to Yuma, why head north after Ajo?'

'Necessity,' Manson said easily. 'You rob small banks, you come away with peanuts. With peanuts, you don't buy prison wardens. Yes, Ajo is small, and so is Gila Bend. But put the pickings from those two small banks in one sack, and who knows?'

Kemp was nodding. 'Then put that sack alongside Guerrero's, and you could be in business.'

'In more than one sense,' Manson said, and again he refused to elaborate when the other two men looked at him quizzically.

'We will come back to that thought,' Guerrero said, 'but for now you must realize that sooner or later a posse will come hunting.'

'Right,' Kemp said. 'And it won't take much of a tracker to spot where we changed course.'

'Which could be bad for you,

Manson,' Guerrero said, 'could ruin all your fine plans for this business or that.'

Manson had his foot hooked up on the horn and was placidly picking his teeth with a splinter of wood.

'That's where men on the run make their big mistake,' he said. 'The first thing gets lodged in their mind is that they're being hunted, and the way they see it a man hunted by a determined posse stands no chance of getting clear. They're wrong.'

'Why wrong, how wrong?' Guerrero said, frowning.

'Because no matter how determined, the posse's always at a disadvantage. A stag at bay's a dangerous beast. The same goes for man. If a man picks his spot, stops running and settles down to wait, before too long he'll find those hunters will run onto his guns.'

'And that is what we do?' Guerrero said, a delighted grin revealing flashing teeth.

'Damn right,' said Manson. 'If they come chasing after us, it won't be too long before they find themselves picking our hot lead from between their teeth.'

And with a broad grin he used a forefinger to flick the makeshift toothpick into the bushes.

★　★　★

It had taken Slade Hawker less than ten minutes to convince the two-man Sasabe council that the posse needed his presence to make their hunt legal, and that the town would survive in his absence. The councillors' reluctant agreement came when he offered to deputize the best two of those men who had failed to make the posse. Accordingly two young, surprised but proud former rejects were summoned, duly sworn in, and within the hour he had specified Hawker, Stanley, Costigan and Mills were riding out of town.

They rode with well-filled saddlebags, with belt and saddle holsters bristling with weapons, and both Morg

Stanley and Wes Costigan were carrying ropes looped on their saddle horns.

Hawker raised no objections. As an officer of the law he was duty bound to bring his brother's killer to trial, yet he knew full well that when a saddle-weary posse runs down hard-bitten outlaws, the situation can easily run out of control and turn ugly. Two of the posse had come prepared, which said something about their philosophy, and their intentions. They would need watching but, that early in the chase, Hawker wasn't giving much thought to how he would react if, in the heat of the moment, Will's killer ended up standing on a horse with a rope around his neck with Stanley or Costigan behind the horse with raised quirt.

At such a time, he speculated, a moment's hesitation could take the decision out of his hands and leave a man's life hanging by the proverbial thread; and that intriguing thought gave him enough macabre amusement to twist his lips in a thin smile.

'They turned,' Costigan said. 'Looks like they're heading north-west.'

He was a wiry, long-haired man wearing a floppy felt hat, range clothes and stovepipe boots. He was hanging half out of the saddle and holding the dun pony with one hand as he scrutinized the hard ground.

'You sure?'

'Yeah. Kinda leaves me flummoxed. I figured this posse was a complete waste of effort, those *hombres*'d cross the border a ways before Nogales and be beyond our reach. Seems I was wrong.'

The three horses had come together, circling as Costigan studied the ground. Now they were standing, not yet blown but already flecked with lather. Absently, Hawker patted his mount's slick neck.

'Riding that way, they're circling back around Sasabe and they've gained no time,' he reasoned. 'They're carrying stolen money. They've turned their backs on safety. Why? Where are they heading?'

In days gone by, old Arn Mills had

spent time with the Texas Rangers. Hunting Apaches had given him a deep knowledge of the South-west. His bony frame was slouched in the saddle, his brow furrowed in thought.

'That direction,' he said, 'there's a whole lot of nothing much. In twenty miles the mountains rise to seven thousand feet at Baboquivari Peak. 'Less those fellers're heading for Casa Grande, they'll be keeping south of those peaks. Biggest town in that more southerly direction's Ajo — hundred miles from here.'

Hawker was frowning. 'Why go there?'

'Rob another bank?'

'But why Ajo? Why not go for Casa Grande, Gila Bend — or Phoenix?'

Morg Stanley, grey-haired and tooth-less but with wise eyes and steady hands, spat into the dust.

'Because Ajo,' he said, 'happens to be on the line they're takin' as they ride to where it is they're agoin'.'

'And where's that?' Hawker said.

'Yuma,' Arn Mills said.

'Why?'

'Border town, river crossing. If they don't like the look of Mexico, California's the next best bet. Crossing the Colorado at Yuma, by steamer or the Southern Pacific Railroad, puts them out of our reach same as the Mex border not a couple of miles from here would — and I hear the climate's real nice by the sea.'

'And if they do pick up extra cash on the way — at the Ajo bank, maybe even in Yuma itself before they make the crossing — they'll have a tidy pile to set up a new life.' Hawker looked at the others, and shook his head doubtfully. 'Is that what you fellers think's going on? It's a fine story, but I tell you now, I can't see it.'

Costigan was looking sceptical.

'Me neither. We're suggesting those owlhoots have got brains, and I never did meet one yet who could count without using his fingers.' He grinned. 'Maybe California's a dream Morg and

Arn have been hankering after for themselves, but right now there's no point in thinking one way or the other. We know which way those galoots are headed. Why look for reasons? We foller 'em, catch 'em, hang a killer from the nearest tall tree. All we're doin' here is wasting time talking.'

Hawker grunted agreement.

'Those bank robbers were barrellin' out of Sasabe almost an hour before you were sworn in. It took another hour to get your old bones movin'. Add on the fifteen minutes we've been sitting here jawin' and they've got more than a twenty mile jump on us.'

'And that,' Mills said gloomily, 'could take us a full day's riding to close down.'

'Then let's get moving,' Hawker said.

'We'll do that, sure, it's your call and that's what we're out here for,' Mills said, 'but first I'd like to get something clear — something we've been talking about.'

He looked at Costigan, and Stanley,

saw their almost imperceptible nods of assent.

'For you, Hawker, this is about much more than a bank robbery,' he went on. 'Your brother was shot dead by one of these varmints. Nobody would blame you if you went a little loco when we do catch up with them, decided to take the law into your own hands, so to speak — if that makes sense, you being a lawman and all.' He grimaced, his embarrassment plain for all to see. 'What I'm tryin' to say, I guess, is that if something like that should happen then you can rely on us to be lookin' in the other direction — '

'I appreciate the thought,' Hawker said. 'My brother and I weren't close, but there's still a great sense of loss . . . ' He smiled. 'Funny thing is, I've already been through the hypothetical situation you've just described, Arn — only I had you fellers down as the ones making the decision to operate outside the law.' He watched them, registered their shock, and said, 'What it amounts to is, we watch each other. That way, when this chase is done, three men get a fair trial, four men can return to normal life with clear consciences.'

He let those words sink in, then touched his horse with his heels. As it moved out onto the trail he looked over his shoulder and made one more comment he felt was necessary in the unusual circumstances.

'Not a whole lot of what we've been discussing makes sense,' he said, as the others pulled alongside and, for a while, they rode in line abreast. 'Me, I can't ever recall outlaws acting in this way. That suggests to me that these fellows really are more intelligent than your usual bunch of drifting owlhoots — despite Costigan's doubts. So, as they've already presented us with the unexpected, keep your wits about you and look for more of the same. And remember this: if they've finished playing games, the next surprise they come up with is likely to carry a sting in the tail that could prove fatal.'

Those words, conveying a stark message that each man knew to be true, seemed to cast a grey pall over the posse. For the next half-hour or so, little was said as each man rode immersed in thoughts that ranged from gloomy misgivings to a fatalistic willingness to accept whatever the gods might throw their way.

It was, not surprisingly, the former Texas Ranger, Arn Mills, who broke the silence. He had for some time been twisting in the saddle as he rode, his sharp eyes constantly ranging along their back trail. Now he turned, faced front, and spat emphatically.

'Don't nobody look now,' he said, 'but there's two riders follering us. They picked up our trail soon's we swung north-west to chase those outlaws. They've been holding steady, maybe a mile back, ever since.'

5

The guards escorted Ben Manson to the warden's office in the Yuma Penitentiary at midday and left him standing in front of the desk dressed in drab prison clothing and wearing waist and ankle chains. They waited outside. Both guards carried shotguns.

Manson was amused, but also burning with curiosity. He spent his days locked in a prison cell because one fateful night in Tombstone he had slipped up badly. Following orders, he had watched a man for most of the evening, then followed him out of the Eagle saloon and shot him in the back. The man had died instantly. But, in the hours spent watching him, Manson had foolishly drunk too much strong liquor. Instead of walking away when the man dropped dead in the dust of the street he had stepped back into the shadows and, with difficulty, rolled a cigarette. The light of the match he struck had been flaring, lighting the half smile on his drunken features, when a deputy town marshal had walked up to him and placed the muzzle of a cocked six-gun to his head.

So far he had fretted and fumed about that mistake, and about the deathly silence from the world outside the jail, for a full ninety days. Nothing had happened to break the routine of prison life — until now.

The blazing Arizona sun was streaming through the window. Hogg, the overweight, balding warden, was sitting behind his desk watching Manson with contempt gleaming in moist eyes almost lost in folds of pale flesh. A cigar smouldered between fat fingers. Ash flaked the front of his dark shirt.

'Who paid you to kill Hainsworth?' Hogg said, managing in those six words to take Manson completely by surprise.

'Paid *me*?' Manson said, gaping. 'I got drunk and made a bad mistake, so

I'd say it's me doin' the paying.'

'You know who he was, what he was?'

'I told you, there was nobody else involved — '

'Hainsworth,' Hogg said impatiently. 'You aware who it was you shot dead?'

Manson shrugged. 'Some old feller who got in the way when I was letting rip with my brand new '75 Remington 'Outlaw' six-gun — '

'You did it deliberate.'

'No, sir. I didn't even see the man.'

'Hainsworth was boss of just about the biggest business in Tombstone. The Silver Lode Mining Company. That was his baby. By plugging him, you took away the brains and left the company floundering.'

Manson nodded sagely. 'Yeah, I can see why I'd want to do that. I plug this Hainsworth, ruin a company I'd never heard of, put myself in jail for twenty-five years. Just about the best decision I ever took — '

'Quit fooling,' Hogg said. 'You knew who he was, eyewitnesses swear you followed him out of the Eagle and shot him in the back.'

'For what? For this?' Manson lifted his hands, chains jingling, and swept them to indicate the prison cells that lay on the other side of the office walls.

'It wasn't intended to end this way. You said you got drunk and made a mistake. So tell me: if you'd been stone cold sober and vanished into the night leaving Hainsworth lying dead on the corner of Fifth and Allen — what then? With Hainsworth dead, what was supposed to happen, Manson?'

'I don't know what you're talking about.'

'All right, for the sake of argument let me tell you what keen observers expected to happen. Let's say — again for the sake of argument — that you plugged Hainsworth to get him out of the way. With Hainsworth dead, the Silver Lode Mining Company was a headless chicken. Within days of his death somebody — let's say the somebody who put you up to killing

71

Hainsworth — should have moved in. Taken over the company. But that didn't happen. So what went wrong?'

'It's your story. You tell me.'

'Somebody,' Hogg said, 'ran short of cash. The man behind the killing, the man who had every intention of taking over the Silver Lode Mining Company, ran short of cash.'

Manson grinned. 'I know the feeling.'

'Which makes me wonder,' Hogg said, viciously mashing the cigar butt in an ashtray already full to overflowing, 'how that somebody — assuming, of course it's the same feller — has managed after a mere ninety days to come up with the wherewithal to secure your release.'

'Wherewithal,' Manson said absently, his heart suddenly pounding in his chest. 'Is that what it takes to bribe a prison warden?'

For an instant he thought he'd gone too far. Crimson suffused the warden's face. The eyes glaring at him through slits had a steely sheen. Fat hands resting on the polished desk top had clenched into white-knuckled fists.

Then Hogg let his breath go in an explosive gust.

'Carter, Evans,' he roared, 'get in here now and get this vermin out of my office.'

He sat back, glowering as the two guards rushed in and bundled the chained man out into the corridor. The door slammed. For some time he stared at the panels. Gradually, the fists relaxed, the unhealthy blood drained from his face. And then, gradually, he began to smile. The smile grew into a broad grin, and suddenly Warden Hogg was laughing, spittle spraying from his thick lips as he threw back his head and roared on and on without control as one meaty fist pounded the desk.

6

By noon on that first day, Clyde Manson was feeling the strain. Unlike his two companions he was not born to the saddle, and several hours' hard riding in the searing heat of an Arizona summer's day had sapped his energy and made thinking clear thoughts nigh on impossible. The blazing sun was almost directly overhead, burning down from a sky that appeared pure white from horizon to horizon. Beneath it, in every direction and as far as the eye could see, the rugged landscape shimmered sickeningly in the heat. To avoid the gritty dust kicked up by their horses, the three riders were forced to pull bandannas up over their sweating faces and ride abreast, many yards apart. Clothing stuck to damp skin. Manson, desperately thirsty, emptied his canteen of precious lukewarm water in the first couple of hours.

Yet for all his distress he did manage to scrape around and come up with a single crumb of comfort. He, Manson, was the man with brains honed on the New York stock exchange and the vision to see business opportunities in a barren, sun-baked territory. Guerrero and Kemp were experienced Westerners, and it was they who would see him through what was unlikely to be more than a few days of intense discomfort.

Nevertheless, what began to concern him more and more as the day wore on and the sheer scale of the distances still to be faced sank in was the growing belief that his planning had been flawed from the start; that enduring a long and tortuous journey prior to this ride across southern Arizona — just so that he could begin his campaign in Sasabe — had been a serious mistake. He knew why he had done it: infuriated and frustrated by massive financial losses that had left him virtually penniless, obsessed with the desire for revenge against the man who had put his younger brother in prison, he had for weeks envisaged the rifle in his hands spurting flame, Marshal Slade Hawker's bloodied body sinking to the ground in front of him with a bullet in the chest. He was an Easterner, and though he was not accustomed to drawing a six-gun from a holster with lightning speed he was an expert shot with both rifle and revolver. But to turn that vision of Slade Hawker's demise into reality he had embarked on a railroad journey clear across Texas to El Paso, joined forces there with Hoss Kemp and taken the Wells Fargo coach to Nogales where Guerrero had met them with three horses and the necessary supplies.

Shouldn't have done it, Manson thought now, head swimming as he eased his weight in the saddle. Should have robbed a bank closer to Yuma — and he chuckled aloud at that thought, then clamped his mouth shut in vague alarm as he detected a note of delirium and saw both Kemp and Guerrero flick a glance in his direction.

Should have . . . what? He shook his head as the thoughts that had been clear in his mind spun away and eluded his grasp. As he shook his head, he rocked in the saddle. Again the chuckle came bubbling from his lips. He sensed Kemp pulling in from the side, riding close enough for their stirrups to click together. Grinning, Manson turned to face him, leaned over and at the same time reached out with a hand.

At that moment, when what little attention he was capable of was distracted and his weight was pulling him sideways — his horse stepped in a prairie dog's burrow and snapped a foreleg.

The crack was sickening. The horse went down with a squeal, throwing Manson sideways out of the saddle. His head hit Kemp's knee. He grabbed for a handhold, missed, and fell heavily to the ground. Something crunched in his shoulder. Pain drew a sharp yelp from his open mouth. Then momentum carried him over in a roll. He finished up face down in the dust, spluttering and spitting.

Manson rolled onto his back and sat up, wiping his mouth. He stayed there, knees up, one hand clutching his shoulder, then watched in dismay as Guerrero rode in from the flank, stepped out of the saddle, drew his six-gun and shot Manson's horse in the forehead. The animal twitched once, then lay still.

'And now we're in deep trouble,' Kemp said.

He was standing in the dry dust, digging his canteen from his saddle-bag and watching over his shoulder as Guerrero put away his pistol. He took a long drink, then grimaced and tossed the canteen to Manson.

'Two horses, three men, one of them *lesionado*,' Guerrero said, looking critically at Manson as he favoured his shoulder. 'You still say we ride a hundred miles to Ajo, rob another bank? I think not, not any more we don't.'

'Count the money,' Manson said.

'Count — '

'Take that sack out of your saddle-bag, see what we've got. A rough count, savvy? An estimate, *una estimación*. When we know how much money we took from the Sasabe bank, then we can work out how best to proceed.'

'We'd best proceed by gettin' the hell out of here,' Kemp said.

'No sense acting hasty — '

'Oh, man, that posse riding hard on our heels'd just *love* listening to you. You want to sit there waiting for a bunch of angry men to come riding in with ropes, that's your affair. Me, I'd prefer to put as many miles as possible between us and them.'

'And so we will,' Manson said.

He climbed awkwardly to his feet, drank from Kemp's canteen, then returned it with a nod of thanks. In some strange way the fall had cleared his head. His thirst was still unquench-able, the realization that he had been making too many mistakes for too long even more intense, but his thinking was clearer than it had been for . . . well, since the terrible day when brother Ben had been convicted of murder and carted away to the Yuma Penitentiary. And that explained the new clarity of thought, Manson realized: it was all down to the relief he felt now that he had settled his score with Marshal Slade Hawker. He was not a violent man, and there had been a welling sickness within him as he pulled the trigger, saw the bullet strike home and watched the man go down in the dust of Sasabe's main street. But with the deed done, with the physical act of killing fading into the background, there was a sense of satisfaction that was almost heady. The deed was done. Marshal Slade Hawker had paid with his life. He was dead.

Guerrero was down on one knee, hastily counting bundles of bank notes he'd dragged out of the sack and piled in the dust. Kemp had strolled some way away and was staring down their back trail, one hand lifted to shade his eyes as he squinted into the distance.

The Mexican sat back on his heels and looked at Manson. His liquid dark eyes were glinting.

'Is a lot,' he said. 'Maybe fifteen thousand dollars, perhaps more, I think.'

Manson took a deep breath. Eyes narrowed, he totted up the cash he needed and mentally weighed that sum against Guerrero's estimate. Even looked at optimistically — there was nowhere near enough. But with a posse certainly closing in while they stood talking and likely to catch up very quickly indeed with Manson forced to ride double with Guerrero or Kemp . . .

'Forget Ajo,' Manson said. 'Guerrero, you figure we can make better time to Yuma taking a more southerly route?'

'For sure. Maybe even we cross the border into Mexico, thumb our noses at the posse if they get too close.'

'Now there's a thought,' Kemp said, grinning. 'If we stay south of the border the whole of the way until San Luis we'll be out of reach of the posse; when we're forced to cross the border again, we'll be within twenty miles of Yuma.'

Manson grunted his approval.

'Riding on Guerrero's home territory, we should also be able to pick up a horse.'

The Mexican grinned. 'No problem,' he said. 'Like I say before this — '

'Yeah, I know,' Kemp cut in, returning Guerrero's grin, 'we do it that way the whole damn business *es fácil*.'

It was with Kemp that Manson rode double, and in that manner an hour's steady riding on a south-westerly course saw them make good progress towards the border. It was the right move, yet Manson felt frustrated, and irritable. It seemed that once again his thinking had been flawed, his plans made in haste. They had been much closer to the border when they rode out of Sasabe. If they had made the crossing then, they would have been in Mexico, and safe, before the Sasabe deputy marshal who had taken over from the late Slade Hawker had time to swear in his posse. Instead, a morning's riding had taken them many miles in what an accident had proved was the wrong direction, and clawing those miles back was slowing down their forward progress. They were cutting across country trying to make the border. A posse travelling in a straight line would be closing fast — had almost certainly been doing so for most of the morning. If that was so, then they were now dangerously close, and several times in that first hour Manson had to physically restrain himself from glancing nervously over his shoulder.

His restraint was not shared by Guerrero.

The Mexican allowed Kemp to lead the way, knowing that the pace must be set by the horse bearing the double load. So Guerrero took up the rear, and with it the responsibility for keeping a watchful eye on the pursuit. In truth, not one of the three men expected the posse to get close enough to trouble them before they reached the border, so it was with a real sense of shock that Kemp and Manson were pulled to an abrupt halt by the Mexican's shouted warning.

Kemp had topped a rise which gave him and Manson a clear view north and south. The morning's riding had carried them sixty miles towards Ajo, the sudden change of direction was taking them towards a border crossing at a point that would put them in line with the 4,000 foot peak of Cerro Cubabi.

'From their vantage point, that mountain was now clearly visible. As Kemp eased his tired horse to a halt, the two men were jubilant. Safety was within a couple of miles. They would cross the border, pick up a horse from one of Guerrero's numerous relatives, and enjoy a spicy Mexican meal before pushing on towards Yuma.'

'*Tener cuidado,*' Guerrero called. 'You two, pay attention, I see what I think is the posse.'

'Jesus!' Manson said, and without

giving a thought to his damaged shoulder he slid from Kemp's horse and ran back to where Guerrero had turned his mount to gaze intently down their back trail.

'Get down,' Manson roared, flapping his hands. 'If you can see them, they can see you.'

'Not for a while yet,' Guerrero said. 'I see dust, I see movement, that is all — but I know it is them. Nevertheless, there is plenty of time for us to set up a reception committee — is that correct? A *comisión de recepción*? This rise stretches east and west. They are forced to cross it. So now we drop below the crest with our horses, then return on foot with our rifles. And then, from the cover here which consists of trees and the high ground itself, we pick them off.'

For a moment Manson hesitated, beset by the doubts that had been plaguing him for most of the day. Then he shrugged. In his financial affairs in New York, Manson had learned to use the resources at his disposal. The Mexican was on home territory. Kemp was a Westerner born and bred. Both men were accustomed to dealing with such situations, and were skilled with the weapons they carried: he had the resources at his disposal.

'We'll do that,' he said. 'Remember what I told you: *If a man picks his spot, stops running and settles down to wait, before too long he'll find those hunters will run onto his guns.* Well, we've picked our spot, and the time is now. Let's take that posse apart.'

7

Not surprisingly, it was sharp-eyed Arn Mills who spotted the vultures circling high in the searing skies and, ten minutes later, saw the dead horse lying in a hollow beneath a buzzing swarm of black flies. The old ranger cut away from the other members of the posse as they drew rein, used his hat to beat off the insects while he leaned out of the saddle to give the dead animal a cursory examination, and within two minutes he was riding back to the group with his eyes searching the ground for sign.

'Happened no more than a half-hour ago,' he said. 'Trickle of blood from the head wound's still looks sticky. Besides, any longer than a half-hour and those birds would've been down tearing that horse to bits in a bloody frenzy.'

Hawker nodded. 'Then if we're that

close in half a day, those bank robbers have been hanging about, wasting time.' He jerked his head at the dead horse. 'What happened there?'

'Stepped in a hole, broke a leg. Nothing they could do for it.' Mills shrugged. 'But what that accident did is give them a big problem, and their plans have changed.'

'How?'

'We figured they were heading for Ajo, then on to Yuma and California — and, yeah, maybe they were,' he went on forcefully as Costigan shook his head. 'But the loss of a horse has slowed them down. Over that kind of distance, two of 'em riding double, we'd run 'em down for sure. From the sign, I'd say they've opted for safety and're makin' a run for the border.'

'I'll second that,' Costigan said. He was down off his horse and had been strolling about studying the hard ground. 'Two horses, one of 'em carrying double, both headin' almost due south.'

'And the border's how far from here?'

'Thirty miles?'

Hawker nodded. 'They make it into Mexico, we're done for. But I think we stand a chance — just.' He flicked a glance back the way they had come, then addressed Arn Mills. 'What about those riders you spotted on our tail? You seen them again?'

Mills nodded. 'Not as close as they were, but I'd say they're still there. A couple of times I saw a flash that could have been reflection; a man watching us through glasses.'

Hawker smiled bleakly. 'I've got a pretty good idea who one of them is. If I'm, right, he's a stubborn young man and he'll've selected a capable pard to ride with him. The important thing is, those fellows are on our side, and that could come in handy if we do hit trouble.'

'Not likely to do that,' Costigan said drily, 'if we set here jawin'.'

'Damn right,' Hawker said, and without waiting for the others he swung his horse and set off at a fast canter towards the Mexican border.

* * *

The nature of the terrain in that part of southern Arizona had been helpful to generations of Apaches, and it was helpful to Nathan Creed and Charlie Birrel. There was always a ridge, bluff or saddle within easy riding distance from which they could gain an elevated viewpoint, and it was from one of those that Birrel detected the posse's abrupt change of direction.

He came slipping and sliding down from the rocky hogback spitting dust and with his brilliant blue eyes alight.

'Heading south,' he said, brandishing his ancient field-glasses. 'Now why would they do that?'

'Could have something to do with those circling vultures I've been watching,' Nathan Creed said, and Birrel nodded.

'A while back I thought I heard a single shot.'

'I've been wondering about that. So far even those glasses of yours haven't brought us a sight of the bank robbers. I'd guess the posse still hasn't got those owlhoots within rifle range, so what we heard wasn't a wild shot loosed off in the hope of downing one of them. Which leaves us with the obvious, and out in the desert a single shot usually means one thing.'

'Three's a cry for help, a single shot usually means an animal's down,' Birrel said, 'which explains the vultures and the change of direction.'

Nathan, absently ridding his black hat of dust by slapping it against his thigh, nodded agreement. 'If it's an outlaw horse that's down, those bank robbers are doing what they should've done in the first place: they're running for the border.'

'Then now's the time,' Birrel said, 'for us to make good use of the angles.'

Creed kept his face straight. If the gunsmith had hoped to confuse him, he was about to be disappointed.

'Ain't that long since I was at school,' he said, 'and I was pretty damn good at geometry.' He hunkered down and sketched a right-angled triangle in the sand. 'Instead of wasting time following those two short legs,' he said, using his finger to trace the lines on either side of the right angle, 'we ride down the long one — the hypotenuse, that's called — and, with luck, intercept the posse before it's too late.'

Birrel was watching him closely.

'You mind explaining that? Too late for what?'

'Too late to save 'em,' Nathan Creed said. 'If I've got the landscape clear in my head, angles and distances and suchlike, Hawker and his posse'll catch up with those bank robbers before they reach Mexico. If I can work that out, so can those owlhoots — and my guess is they're going to be looking for the right place to set up an ambush.'

★ ★ ★

Twelve miles in an hour on horseback is good riding at the best of times. In the Arizona desert conditions are rarely ideal, and Hawker knew that the outlaws would never manage that pace, over rugged terrain, in merciless heat, with one horse carrying double. Yet, despite those extraordinary difficulties, he knew it was still possible for desperate outlaws to reach the border ahead of the posse, and if they did, then all was lost. So Hawker pushed the posse brutally, punishing both horses and men in his efforts to bridge the gap between posse and outlaws before it was too late.

In retrospect, when he looked back on events, he would be forced to admit that he had gone for speed at the expense of caution; had pushed on blindly instead of studying changing conditions and adjusting the speed and direction of the chase accordingly.

For the first few miles, his adherence to blind pursuit was no cause for concern. The posse was traversing baked flatlands, the sun beating down on them as they rode almost flat out in an extended line with dust flaring behind them like wind-blown smoke from a mile-wide scrub fire. Ahead of them, as far as the eye could see before being thwarted by the shimmering heat haze, visibility was unobstructed. The three old-timers were in high spirits, reliving the wild days of their youth as they stretched out on their racing mounts. The wind was flattening their hat brims. There was fire in their old eyes, a fierce coursing of blood through their veins as excitement caught them in its grip and refused to let go.

Then, just as the sheer effort of keeping going at speed was sapping the strength and will of horses and men and causing the heady excitement to wane, high ground came into view. It revealed itself gradually, first as a smudge that on another day might have been banks of distant cloud, then as a recognizable ridge that stretched east and west, reached a height of perhaps

200 feet and was topped in places by parched trees.

'Only way round,' Hawker called from the flank, 'is if we turn east and waste time making a big half circle.'

'No point,' Costigan said. 'Quickest way's over the top. My guess is we're closing in. From up there I reckon we'll get a clear sight of those pesky bank robbers.'

'If we see 'em, and they're nearing the border,' Arn Mills said, 'there's only the one way of stopping them.'

'Bring them down, using rifles,' Hawker said. 'If that's what it takes, that's what we'll do,' and he spurred his tired horse forward and put it to the rising ground.

★ ★ ★

The lie of the land and the direction Creed and Birrel had taken down what Creed had called the triangle's hypotenuse meant that they approached the ridge stretching roughly east to west not from its northern side, but from its eastern end where it petered out and sloped down to the flat plains. This gave the two riders a peculiar advantage: as they rode in they could see along both the north and south slopes.

It was Creed who, attracted by the flash of sunlight on bright metal, spotted the dust cloud and ahead of it the black dots that were the four riders of the posse making for the ridge's northern slope. At once he called out to Birrel who was some fifty yards ahead.

'Caught 'em,' he yelled. 'What do we do, let 'em know we're here, or stay backed off?'

Birrel looked where Creed was pointing, then lifted his hand to show he'd seen the riders and slowed his horse to let the youngster catch up.

'I'm puzzled,' he said. 'The border's no more than five miles to the south of the ridge. The posse's coming in from the north, if they're still riding hard then they're still behind the outlaws. That means those galoots must be over the top and riding like bats out of hell. Beyond the ridge, the terrain's flat desert. If a jack-rabbit pops its head up out of a hole, I'd see it — but even with the glasses I can't see those outlaws.'

'A man can't sneeze in this part of the world without kicking up a mess of dust,' Creed said. 'No dust means — '

'No riders,' Birrel finished for him. 'Yet we know they're there.'

'We know they're somewhere,' Creed said. 'But maybe Hawker got it wrong. Maybe he turned the posse south, when the bank robbers continued to push west.'

Birrel shook his head.

'I read it right, and Hawker got it right. Vultures were circling because a horse was down. We can both see four riders in the posse, so it must have been an outlaw horse. Forced to ride double, they'd change plan and head for the border.'

'So where are they?'

'If they're not there in front of the posse,' Birrel said, 'and they're not beyond the ridge heading for the border, then there's only one place they can be.'

'Up there on the ridge,' Creed said softly. 'In the trees. Doing exactly what we said they would.'

'Setting up an ambush.'

'Climb down, get your glasses out, Charlie, and see what you can see. There's trees up there, and they'll use them for cover, but those fellers are hiding from the posse, not from us.'

For most of what was now almost a day's ride from Sasabe, Nathan Creed had been feeling antagonistic towards Marshal Slade Hawker — if he thought of him at all. But with the clear certainty that the man was now in danger, he was aware that his feelings had changed. This, after all, was the man who had rescued Nathan's mother from a miserable life tied to a violent man. Mollie Creed had gone willingly with the tall lawman. Alexander Creed had cared so little for his wife he had not even bothered to go after her.

His ma, Nathan realized, was better off now than she had been for many years. But now the man who had brought a measure of comfort into her life was riding straight into the guns of a trio of outlaws turned bushwhackers.

'Damn it,' Nathan said softly, and as Charlie Birrel stood with his legs braced and the field-glasses to his eyes he let his horse roam in a restless circle, from time to time flicking his gaze towards the four racing horsemen who were drawing ever closer to the ridge. One, the leading rider, was even now approaching the lower slopes.

'I see 'em,' Charlie Birrel said suddenly.

'Doin' what?'

'What you'd expect. Horses are hobbled. All three men are down, letting that posse get real close before they open up on them. It'll be a bloody massacre.'

'We were talking earlier about the meaning of shots in the desert, weren't we? Well, let's hope they understand

what I'm trying to tell them with these,'
Nathan Creed said and, without waiting for a reply, he drew his six-gun,
pointed it towards the limitless skies
and fired three shots in rapid succession.

★　★　★

To the members of the posse, the sound
of shots coming from the east was
disorientating enough to leave them
momentarily stunned.

Hawker couldn't comprehend what
was happening. They were riding on
the ridge's lower slopes. It was their
intention to reach the top and from
there look down on the fleeing outlaws
and either continue the pursuit, or
bring them down.

Now, the volley of shots coming from
their left flank suggested they'd walked
into a trap. If it was a trap, then it
would be a pincer movement. The next
attack would come from their *right*
flank.

It took but a fraction of a second for those thoughts to race through Hawker's mind. Then, acting instinctively, he turned towards the source of the shots. Two riders were bearing down on them. They were a quarter of a mile away. Metal glinted in their fists.

'Costigan, Stanley,' Hawker roared, 'take care of those two. Mills, you come with me.'

Hawker swung his horse to the right, saw Mills do the same — and was at once appalled to hear the sharp crackle of rifle fire *coming from the top of the ridge*.

Wrenching his horse to a halt, he looked up the slope. As he did so, he heard the solid thump of a bullet hitting flesh, heard Mills grunt deep in his throat. Hawker turned. Mills was down, flat on his back, his foot caught in a stirrup. His horse ran a few yards, then stopped, eyes rolling, ears flat.

His mind a whirl, Hawker again turned his horse. As his frantic gaze sought out Costigan and Stanley he had the weird sensation of being locked in a crazy dance on horseback. He had been wrong. The three outlaws were in cover, on top of the ridge. The hiss and whine of bullets was all around him. He was exposed and there was nowhere he could hide. If he turned to flee, his back would be inviting a bullet. If he couldn't hide, or run, and dare not remain where he was, then then only option left to him was attack. Gritting his teeth, he again turned his mount and pointed it up the slope.

Before the tired horse could answer Hawker's call on its reserves of strength, a bullet drilled into the gallant animal's skull with a vicious crack. Its forelegs buckled. It went down then rolled sideways on the slope. Hawker was tossed from the saddle. He landed flat on his back. All the breath was driven from his body. He rolled, gasping, fought his way to his knees. On all fours, he gazed with bleary eyes to where he had last seen Costigan and Stanley.

On the slope, two bodies lay without moving. Two horses with trailing reins were trotting away from the downed men and up towards the crest of the ridge. As Hawker watched, a swarthy man with a sombrero flying from its neck cord emerged from the trees and ran to the horses. He swept up the loose reins in one fist, then leaped onto Costigan's horse. Leading Stanley's horse, he leaned forward in the saddle and rode furiously back towards the trees. As he did so, Arn Mills's horse got caught up in the excitement and, empty stirrups flapping, deserted its dead rider and raced up the hill after the outlaw.

Still on his knees, swearing with what breath he could muster, Hawker slapped his hand to his holster. It was empty. Despairingly, he watched the moustachioed outlaw reach the trees and disappear from view.

A rattle of shots snapped his gaze back down the slope. The two riders hammering in from the east had covered that last quarter-mile. One of them had tumbled from his horse, found a convenient boulder and was sprawled behind it blasting away with a Winchester at the hidden outlaws.

He wore a black hat. Silver conchos glittered in the sun.

Nathan Creed.

Hawker closed his eyes, let his weight rest on his braced arm, fought to regain his breath. When he opened his eyes again he saw Sasabe's gunsmith, Charlie Birrel, contemptuously ignoring the bullets that were kicking up dirt at his feet. The broad-shouldered man stepped fearlessly down from his horse and walked first to Wes Costigan, then to Morg Stanley.

Then he straightened, looked across at Hawker and shook his head.

'Both gonners,' he called.

Even as he spoke, as if a blanket had been dropped over them the rifles up on the ridge fell silent. Nathan Creed tilted the barrel of his rifle towards the sky, and stood up. He called out gleefully to Hawker.

'Got one of 'em,' he cried. 'Saw him drop. Thought maybe I got a second, but two have lit out so I could be wrong.'

Wearily, his throat dry, his chest a solid ache, Hawker climbed to his feet. Through the coarse grass the two men left standing in the fading haze of gunsmoke came together slowly. There was a dead horse behind Hawker, the body of Arn Mills further up the hill. A little way across the ridge's steep slope the bodies of Costigan and Stanley were further mute testimony to the accuracy of the outlaws' shooting.

And the kid was right, Hawker realized: the barely audible murmur of hoofs as the fleeing outlaws descended the far side of the ridge sounded, to Hawker, like a ghostly kettle drummer mockingly beating out the time for his own, laboured retreat. For what else could he do? His posse had been ripped apart by the outlaws' bullets. The outlaws had lost a man, but those remaining had three spare horses and they were racing towards the border. In the space of less than five minutes of furious gunfire, the situation had been reversed. Hawker's horse was dead. With the arrival of Charlie Birrel and Nathan Creed he still had men to ride with him, but he would be forced to ride double with one of them, inevitably slowing down the chase.

The outlaws could not be caught.

The manhunt was over.

8

'If you're right,' Nathan Creed said, 'we don't need to catch them. If they're heading for Yuma, then California, we make for the nearest town with a telegraph office and wire ahead. If we can't stop them, then it'll be up to the Yuma marshal.'

'What I'd like to know,' Charlie Birrel said, looking with some perplexity at Hawker, 'is where this idea came from. What the hell makes you think they're heading for California?'

'I'm not saying I do think that — not for sure,' Hawker said. He thought back to the talking that had been done on the trail and said, 'It was a notion raised by Arn Mills and Morg Stanley. At the time, I disagreed. But it seems to me that if they were right, then by crossing the border those outlaws are making it easier for themselves. Legally, once they're in Mexico we can't touch them.'

'How about illegally?' Nathan Creed said.

Hawker pulled a face, hating to put the kid down.

'I gave those old-timers my opinion on a similar contentious issue. We vowed to watch each other, make sure nobody stepped out of line. Same applies here: we stay on the side of the law. Besides, if we did cross the border that could put us up against the *rurales*.'

'Could do it by accident,' Nathan said. 'Far as I can see, it's open to individuals to decide exactly what marks the Mex' border. There's no fence, no marker posts, no line drawn in the sand. Easy for a man to make an honest mistake. And forget the *rurales*. They're too busy chasing bandits and posing in those fancy grey uniforms with all that silver braid to pay us any attention.'

The three men were bare-headed and sweating freely as they sat in the shade of the trees on the flat crest of the ridge. Around them spent cartridge cases glittered in the sun, testimony to the volume of fire the outlaws had poured down on the hopelessly exposed posse. Several yards away, four mounds of fresh earth piled with rocks indicated where Morgan Stanley and Arn Mills were buried alongside the grave of the bank robber downed by Nathan Creed.

Digging those four graves in the bone-dry earth had taken almost three hours. Even then the holes were so shallow that the thin covering of earth was insufficient to protect the bodies from marauding animals, and a further half-hour had been spent carrying rocks up and down the steep slope.

Before they buried the Mexican, Charlie Birrel had taken a long look at the dead outlaw's face. Then he'd shaken his head: he'd watched the bank robbery and its tragic aftermath, and the dead outlaw was not the man who had shot Will Hawker.

Birrel was sitting with his back against a tree. His Stetson was tipped forward so that his blue eyes were almost lost in shadow.

'Like I said, I saw what happened outside the bank from the window over my workshop,' he said. 'Heard that outlaw who was holding the horses doing some shouting, too — though I couldn't see his face because for most of the time he was looking the other way. He was throwing a question at Will as he walked up the street. And I heard Will answer.'

He planted his Stetson on his head, poked it back with a forefinger. He was looking at Hawker, waiting for the continuation.

'Then I heard the shot, saw the muzzle flash — saw Will go down before I could get anywhere near,' Hawker said bitterly. He sighed. 'This got a bearing on what we're trying to work out here, Charlie?'

'I think it might help you to understand the killer,' Birrel said. 'If you understand him, that could give you an edge.'

'Go on.'

'What this feller shouted was, 'Is your name Hawker?''

'Just that? Hawker?'

'That's it.'

Hawker was sitting with his legs crossed. Alongside him gun-belts were piled in an untidy heap. He had found his own missing six-gun. The other weapons had been taken from the dead men. He listened carefully to what Birrel had to say, then nodded slowly and thoughtfully. And suddenly, as the implication in the gunsmith's words slowly sank home, it was as if a cold hand had clamped on his heart and lungs and begun squeezing the breath from his body.

'Will answering yes to the question only gave half an answer,' he said tightly. 'A first name was needed to tell it all. I think that bank robber jumped to a conclusion, and shot the wrong man.'

Nathan Creed, knowing something of Hawker's background from his relationship with his mother, caught on at once.

'This got something to do with the time you were deputy marshal in Tombstone, under Virgil Earp?'

'I arrested a man, he was convicted and sentenced to twenty-five years in Yuma Penitentiary for the murder of a businessman. That upset his folks — particularly his brother. I never saw the man, but I heard he was coming after me. That's when Sheriff John Behan advised me to leave town and I wound up in Sasabe.'

'If this bank robber is the man who was coming after you,' Charlie Birrel said, 'he shot Will thinking he was killing the man who put his brother in jail — right?'

'From what you overheard, I'm sure of it. He was hunting a man called Hawker. Maybe he knew the first name, maybe he didn't. Either way, it makes me responsible for Will's death.'

'Whoa, hold on a minute,' Charlie Birrel said. 'There's only one man responsible for that crime, and that's the man who gunned down Will.'

'Manson,' Hawker said bleakly, recalling the days in Tombstone. 'The kid I put away for the businessman's murder was Ben; his older brother's Clyde. I've never set eyes on him so, like you, I wouldn't recognize him if he was close enough to buy me a drink.'

For a few minutes there was silence as the three men pondered on what they had pieced together. Nathan Creed had climbed to his feet as Birrel was talking. He was standing on the edge of the trees, the conchos on his hat glittering as gazed towards the Mexican border. Birrel had now tipped his hat forward over his eyes, and to a casual onlooker it would have looked for all the world as if he was dozing.

Hawker knew different. He'd had some dealings with Charlie Birrel in Sasabe, and he knew the gunsmith was a deep thinker. Which, Hawker thought wryly, was more than he could say for himself at that particular moment. Already grieving, the realization that he was at least in part responsible for his brother's death had left him stunned. In addition, when raising his posse he had sworn in three old-timers. All three were dead. All three, he knew, had families.

Suddenly he realized Birrel was watching him.

'If you can manage it,' Birrel said gently, 'look on the bright side. Let's assume we've got this all worked out. That means we not only know why your brother was gunned down, we've got a fair idea why his killer robbed the Sasabe bank, and where he's going.'

Hawker cleared his throat, mentally shook himself, and nodded.

'Yes, it all adds up. The warden at Yuma's a man called Hogg. He's corrupt. Come up with enough cash and he'll do just about anything: get a prisoner killed, allow weapons to be smuggled into the pen — or arrange for a prisoner's early release, with a fake pardon all written out and signed.'

'So doing like Nathan said and telegraphing ahead won't do much good,' Birrel pointed out. 'The warden's the man at the top. If he's corrupt, he'll tear up the wire, collect his cash and let this Ben Manson walk free.'

Hawker nodded agreement. 'True, but that's not my concern. The courts convicted Ben Manson. If Hogg accepts a bribe to set him free, that's something else for the courts to look into — if they smell a rat. But one thing's a sure fire certainty: for that bribe to be handed over, in cash, Clyde Manson has to be there at the Yuma Penitentiary. You got that right: we know exactly where he's going.'

'And he's on his own,' Nathan Creed called. He'd been listening as he gazed into the distance. Now he walked back to join Hawker and Birrel, his eyes alight with pride.

'I thought I'd plugged two of them,' he said. 'We buried one, but the other I thought I'd winged rode away. He didn't get far. I just spotted his horse grazing about half a mile from here.'

'If it's Manson,' Charlie Birrel said, 'it's all over.'

'If it's not,' Hawker said, climbing wearily to his feet, 'the real chase has just begun. Let's go down there and find out if we're going home, or making the long ride to Yuma.'

9

They descended from the ridge in single file, the sun beating down on them and the reek of dust and scorching vegetation in their nostrils as they let the horses pick their way sure-footedly through the saguaro dotting southern slopes that were steeper and more rocky than those facing due north. Despite the salt sweat stinging his eyes, Hawker could see clearly that there was more than one horse in the hazy distance. That was to be expected. If Nathan Creed had put a bullet in a second man, and he was down, then the remaining outlaw had no need of three spare mounts for his solitary ride. He'd left two of them ground tethered and grazing placidly alongside his dead partner. Pushing on with his own horse and one spare would surely see him safely to Yuma.

But he would only be proceeding to Yuma, Hawker reasoned, if that remaining live outlaw was Clyde Manson.

Fifteen minutes later, they had their answer.

'Mexican,' Charlie Birrel said, standing over the dead man lying sprawled in the dust.

'Yeah. When Costigan and Stanley went down, I saw him come running out of the trees after the horses,' Hawker said.

'So did I,' Nathan Creed said. 'I took a bead on him when he was heading back for the trees, loosed two good shots.'

'Both got him in the back,' Birrel said.

'In a space you could cover with a silver dollar,' Creed said proudly. 'Looks like me shooting up Sasabe most Saturday nights finally paid off.'

Hawker rolled his eyes at the kid's shameless bragging, then turned to Birrel.

'The man you saw challenging my

brother in Sasabe's main street,' he said, 'was it this Mexican?'

'No,' Birrel said, 'and if the young man you put in Yuma for murder was a white man then you already know that. Your brother's killer was not the man we buried up on the ridge, and he's not this man.'

'Then the man who got away is Clyde Manson. By now he's crossed the border into Mexico. He'll be riding hard for Yuma, where he'll hand the cash he stole in Sasabe to the corrupt warden of the Penitentiary. When he walks out into the sunshine, his brother will walk with him.'

'And then,' Birrel said, 'he and his brother will either go back over the border into Mexico, or push on west into California.'

Hawker shook his head in despair. He turned to his horse, fumbled in the saddle-bag and pulled out his canteen. When he shook it, he pulled a face.

'Empty.'

Creed dug out his canteen, and

tossed it to Hawker. The marshal wet his lips, drank a single mouthful of the tepid water and returned the canteen with a nod of thanks.

'On the other side of the ridge I was on foot, now I've got three horses,' he said. 'If I take a spare and change horses at intervals along the way I can get to Yuma as fast as Manson; I'll be eating his dust as we ride into town; could even get there ahead of him.'

'Me and the kid can make use of the third horse,' Birrel said, flexing his shoulders as he glanced at Nathan Creed. 'You won't find us falling too far behind.'

'I don't even expect you to go with me. I rode out of Sasabe at the head of a posse. Those men are dead. Now it's up to me to see this through.'

'You told me I couldn't be part of that posse,' Nathan Creed said. 'What you said made no difference then, it makes no difference now. And think about this: the two bank robbers were put down by *me* while you were groping about in the grass for your six-gun — '

'That was using a rifle to pick off men from a safe distance,' Charlie Birrel interrupted. 'Facing up to a gunslinger who's no more than thirty feet away in a dusty street when your hands are shaking and your mouth's gone too dry to spit — '

'If that's a picture sends shivers down your spine,' Creed said, 'you'd best turn around and ride home.'

'Not me, sonny. You're here because I invited you along. I can just as easy uninvite you. A man who gets too big for his boots can be a danger to all concerned.'

'Let him be,' Hawker said. 'What you say makes sense, Charlie, but we're wasting time we haven't got. And as we've got around to discussing danger, it's important we understand and accept that Clyde Manson's an unknown. Every time we try to figure out his next move, we're relying on guesswork. We talk about Mexico, we talk about California:

all guesses. We don't know what he's going to do.'

'Or if what he does will be done by him on his own, or with another pack of desperadoes — and if it's that, then you need us,' Nathan Creed said.

'Accepted,' Hawker said, after a moment's thought he acceded was unnecessary. 'You ride with me. Both of you.'

Creed was grinning with delight.

'To Yuma? As deputies?'

'I swore in three men, and lost them all,' Hawker said. 'Are you two willing to take that risk?'

'No man,' Charlie Birrel said with a straight face, 'can be that unlucky twice in one lifetime.'

★　★　★

Clyde Manson rode the 150 miles to Yuma in fifteen hours and left one horse in the Gila Desert, dead from exhaustion, the other hung of head and scarce able to put one foot in front of the other as it carried the bank robber to the gates of the Yuma Penitentiary on a bluff above the Colorado.

Inside, covered by a guard carrying a shotgun, Manson removed the sweat-stained saddle-bags from the wrung-out horse and slung them over his arm. He gave his name. Then he was kept waiting for half an hour in an enclosed area between stone walls that trapped the heat of the blazing sun while another guard was despatched to the warden's office to see if Hogg was available, and willing to talk to the visitor.

'Manson, bone-weary and beaten down by the sun, was having difficulty staying awake and upright. He was coated with the dust of the desert. His tongue felt too big for his mouth. His eyes were red-rimmed and blood-shot. He was kept on his feet only by the knowledge that every minute that passed brought him closer to the reunion with his brother, and that a big chunk of the stolen money weighing down the saddle-bags would buy his brother's freedom. Leaving him, he thought bitterly, not enough. Not *nearly* — '

'All right,' the guard with the shotgun growled. 'He'll see you now.'

He went with Manson, always behind him, never lowering the shotgun. When Manson was admitted to the warden's office, he knew even as the door closed behind him that the guard would keep watch outside.

Let him do that, Manson thought exultantly. Let him watch when Ben is brought in from his cell, let him watch with amazement when he walks out again, a free man.

Hogg, he saw as he approached the desk, was a fat and balding man who was studying him with unconcealed amusement. The smoke from his cigar curled around his glistening face. His eyes were permanently narrowed. His mouth had a cruel twist.

'Well, I made it,' Manson said. 'Not without some difficulty along the way, but here I am.'

'What was the sum we agreed?'

Manson told him.

'You've got it?'

Manson lifted the saddle-bags.

'Show me. Take it out. Put it on the desk.'

Manson stepped forward unsteadily. He unbuckled one bag, dipped his hand inside and felt the bundles of notes. Then he tipped the bag, emptied it onto the desk. He had done the calculations on the trail. Hogg's money was in that one bag. His money, the money he needed, was in the other. It was a rough fifty-fifty split. And it left him short.

Hogg had leaned forward. With one crooked arm he dragged the money across the desk towards him. He dragged it right to the edge. Then he slid open a drawer, dragged the money over the edge of the desk so that it tumbled into the drawer.

He slammed the drawer, and sat back.

'We've got a small problem, Manson.'

Manson sucked in a deep breath. Those few ominous words had made him dizzy. He stared at Hogg, at the eyes deep-set in creased flesh, the cruel mouth.

'You've got your money, Hogg. The sum we agreed. All of it. You try to back out now — '

'I wouldn't do that. Trust me, I'm a man of my word,' Hogg said, and he grinned. 'You paid me. When you leave here, your brother will leave with you.'

Manson dragged a hand across his face, and shivered with relief.

'So . . . what was the problem?'

'There was an altercation in the yard. Your brother was a cocky young feller and that could be an irritation — it got to be more so when he knew he was on his way out. He pushed too hard against a man who wouldn't be pushed.'

Hogg looked down at the glowing end of his cigar. When he looked up again, his gaze was mocking.

'Your brother took a knife in the

belly, Manson. He died last night in the infirmary. I told you he'd leave with you. You can take his body, give him a decent burial.'

Clyde Manson closed his eyes. His mind was numb. The shocking news had taken away the last of the strength that remained after the long ride to Yuma. His knees were trembling. He opened his eyes, leaned forward and took his weight by leaning on the desk.

'I want my money back,' he said hoarsely.

'Get your hands off my desk.'

'I want — '

'You heard me. Stand up.'

Manson straightened up. His mind was racing, but seemed to be proceeding in circles. Ben dead . . . dead . . . He shook his head to clear it, thought about what he had to do, what he needed to clinch what could be his most important business transaction since leaving New York.

'Warden, the deal agreed with you was my brother would be pardoned, and released. That cannot happen. I appreciate that his death had nothing to do with you, but he's dead, that deal cannot be completed, and I want my money.'

'What money?'

'The money I gave — '

'You gave me no money; I took no money.'

'Jesus Christ, I dumped it on the desk, you put it in that drawer.'

'Are you telling me I accepted a bribe?'

'Call it what the hell you like.'

'I'm an honourable man. If you'd tried to bribe me, you'd have discovered to your cost that it doesn't pay. You'd have been marched out of here, thrown in a cell — '

Manson lunged across the desk. His fingers closed on Hogg's shirt. He dragged the man's dead weight towards him. Then Hogg swung a meaty fist. He put his shoulder into the swing. His knuckles cracked against Manson's jaw, knocked him backwards.

'Guard,' Hogg roared. 'Get this man out of my office, take him to his brother, then throw both of them out of my prison.'

* * *

Slade Hawker's best estimate as they rode into Yuma with the setting sun in their eyes was that they were arriving anything up to twelve hours behind Clyde Manson. His gloomy calculations were based on his estimate of the outlaw's progress along the Mexican border if he'd made good use of his spare horse, and the setbacks that had plagued his own desperate race across the Gila Desert.

Fifty miles after burying the dead Mexican bank robber, two of the five horses being ridden by Hawker, Birrel and Creed were too exhausted to continue. Leaving them to die of thirst in the desert was unthinkable. They pushed on. After proceeding at a drastically reduced pace for ten miles, the unofficial posse came across a small homestead nestling in a verdant hollow. The bearded owner waved them in as his woman stood in the cottage doorway with a shotgun in her hand, and was delighted to take the animals off their hands.

Ten miles further on, Hawker's horse went lame. So bad was the leg injury that they were slowed from a fast, ground-eating canter to a painful walking pace and, with eighty miles in front of them, Manson would inevitably pull further and further ahead. Hawker, swearing in frustration, knew they had either to nurse the injured animal all the way to Yuma, or ride back to the homestead and leave it with the lucky homesteader.

Would riding double be faster than nursing the lame horse?

After a brief discussion, Charlie Birrel grimly voiced the sensible third option. A few minutes later, after a swig of whiskey from a bottle Hawker had no idea he was carrying, he put a bullet in the lame horse's brain. They did what they could to hide the carcass from scavenging animals — a task they were becoming accustomed to — then pressed on towards Yuma with Hawker riding double on the lighter Nathan Creed's horse.

They covered the eighty miles in fifteen hours. Both horses were quivering with exhaustion. Stiff and tired, Hawker, Birrel and Creed slid from the saddles like very old men. It was the quiet of the evening. They stood stretching their creaking limbs as the fiery-red skies were changing to the purple of approaching night. All around them oil lamps were being lit.

Their first stop in Yuma's main street was the livery barn where they left the wrung-out horses in the hands of an ancient hostler who looked at their condition and spat his contempt. Their second was a greasy café where they ate their first hot meal since leaving Sasabe. With that packed inside them they stepped out onto the lamp-lit plank walk, let leather belts out a couple of notches, and stood in the lamp-light pondering their next move.

'No sense going to the Penitentiary,' Hawker said. 'We've no connection to Ben Manson, and in Tombstone I spoke out against Hogg too often for him to relax the rules or do me any favours.'

'You're the lawman who arrested Manson, and we're still in Arizona Territory,' Birrel said. 'Doesn't that make you official enough to get information?'

'It may be Arizona, but I'm working under the sheriff of Pima County.'

Creed had wandered away, something Hawker had noticed he had a habit of doing. The restlessness of the young? Insatiable curiosity? Easily bored? All of those, Hawker thought wryly — then he was back on the alert as the youngster turned to him.

'You recognize that horse?'

Creed was pointing across the street. Half-a-dozen horses were hitched outside the saloon. Most had been tied there by riders who had arrived while they were in the café eating their meal. The one Creed was indicating was crusted with dried sweat, stained with trail dust, standing listlessly with its head drooping and its legs braced.

'Maybe,' Hawker said. 'Let's go see.'

He led the way across the street. One swift glance at the weary, dozing horse confirmed what Creed had spotted: the horse had belonged to ex-Texas Ranger, Arn Mills.

'Left there by Clyde Manson,' Charlie Birrel said bluntly. 'That tells us he made it all the way, and it means Arn's horse has probably been standing here in the hot sun for most of the day. Somebody inside must've noticed, maybe knows something — which is convenient,' he said, grinning, 'because my throat's been wondering where the next drink's coming from.'

The night was still young, the saloon dimly lit. Several men were sitting at tables, three engaged in a game of poker with matches as stakes. Hawker,

Birrel and Creed crossed to the bar and ordered beer from a barman with a wall-eye and a dirty towel slung over a thin shoulder. He merely shrugged and walked away when Hawker enquired after Arn Mills's horse, but a man in a dark suit and fancy boots standing drinking a few feet away was more enlightening.

'It's been there since early morning,' he said. 'I've passed by from time to time in the course of my business. Figure the man who left it there must be a heartless son of a gun.'

'You catch sight of him?'

The man nodded. 'Once. A man I was talking to pointed him out, mentioned that he was the owner of the horse. I was about to say something, but his looks and his manner were off-putting. Looked like he'd travelled hard, and wouldn't be averse to using the six-gun he carried on his hip.' He smiled. 'I'm Zeke Ablett. You got a particular interest in that horse, or the man?'

The question was accompanied by a jerk of the head towards the badge pinned to Hawker's vest.

Hawker nodded. 'He's a bank robber, and a killer. He shot down a lawman in Sasabe, Pima County. A posse was raised . . . '

Hawker let his words trail away, knowing he was out of his jurisdiction, reluctant to be too free with his information. He waited while Ablett digested what he'd heard, and nodded to Birrel and Creed. Then, as Birrel ordered drinks and tactfully moved the youngster a few paces away along the bar where he engaged him in conversation, Hawker turned again to Ablett.

'This feller you saw — when was that?'

'Not too long ago. Hour, hour and a half?'

'Damn. We just missed him. Was he alone?'

'No, he was accompanied by a younger man.'

'And they went where?'

Ablett shrugged. 'I can't say, with accuracy. I got the impression they were heading for the Yuma Crossing.' He hesitated. 'They were on foot, but the older man was carrying saddle-bags.'

'I'd be very surprised if he'd left them on that horse,' Hawker said softly.

Ablett nodded. 'I'm beginning to put events together here. Killer, bank robber — saddle-bags that feller hung on to like his life depended on it.' He shook his head. 'If I'm right, he's in California by now. Me, I'm heading in the opposite direction, bound for Tombstone where I'll be *spending* a lot of money.'

Hawker's drink arrived. He tasted the cold beer, closed his eyes for an instant, thought over what Ablett had said. If the businessman was right, Manson and his brother were out of Hawker's reach for good. If that was so, there was no sense in dwelling on the posse's failure. Win or lose, they couldn't bring Will back. When situations became impossible to change, a man should move on . . .

'Tombstone means silver mines to me,' Hawker said.

'To you, to me, and to a lot of serious investors among whom I'm pleased to be numbered,' Ablett said. 'But I need to get in fast, and I'm fretting because, other than on horseback, the quickest way to Tombstone is by stage.'

'Southern Pacific Railroad's transcontinental line went through Benson in March this year,' Hawker said. 'That town's twenty-five miles north of Tombstone. Go by the railroad, buy or rent a horse in Benson, you'd be in Tombstone a couple of hours later — long before the stage gets there.'

Ablett brightened. 'Now that is good advice. Maybe I'll do that.' He cocked an eyebrow at Hawker. 'But how about you, and your posse? With that feller and those saddle-bags he was toting long gone, are you continuing the pursuit?'

Hawker hesitated. He saw that both

Charlie Birrel and Nathan Creed had heard the question and, although they hadn't turned towards him, he knew they were listening hard.

He shook his head at Ablett.

'I don't think so,' he said. 'My jurisdiction ended at the Pima County border and I've been chasing a shadow ever since then. No, a killer got away, the hunt's over: It's time for me and my posse to ride home.'

10

Two days later the man calling himself Zeke Ablett arrived in Tombstone. He stepped down off the Wells Fargo stage carrying his saddle-bags, and within an hour had selected and bought a horse from the nearest livery barn. Still wearing the black suit and fancy boots he had rigged himself out in at the end of his long ride to Yuma and the fiasco with the corrupt prison warden, Hogg, he rode up to the Silver Lode Mining Company on a bare ridge overlooking the town and backed by the San Pedro hills.

He was not impressed with his first sight of the low-slung timber building with the sign outside that proclaimed it as the company's head office. *Only* office, more like it, Ablett thought, then was forced to grin when he realized that a man with a severe shortage of capital couldn't afford to complain.

When he dismounted, tied his horse to the rail and began unbuckling the saddle-bags, the office door was already opening. A man stepped out. Fleshy, florid, wearing a dark suit and string tie, he was looking at Ablett with expectation tinged with a measure of doubt.

'Don't let the trail dust coating my garments put you off,' Ablett said, 'it's what I've got in these saddle-bags that should interest you.'

'You're Midas?'

Ablett grinned. 'Zeke Ablett. The name was my modest attempt at enticement and secrecy — now no longer needed.'

'My name's Dane Swift. Come inside and meet my partners.'

They shook hands, then Swift led the way inside. Ablett swept a glance around the room, took in the parapher-nalia of a working office, the long table, the two men sitting there who had impassively watched his entrance.

Several minutes later the introductions were over, drinks had been poured, and the four men were seated. The three Silver Lode directors sat on one side of the long table. Ablett sat opposite them. The worn leather saddle-bags were on the table in front of him.

'We do have a slight problem,' Ablett said, laying a hand on the bulkier of the two bags and unconsciously echoing the words spoken to him by the warden of Yuma Penitentiary. 'The money's here, as promised, but I've been able to raise only half of what you're expecting.'

'If you've raised only half,' the dour man introduced as Gallagher growled, 'why are you here wasting our time?'

'Half is still a lot of cash. My understanding is you've got none. With my injection of capital, the Silver Lode Mining Company will once again be a going concern.'

'But what you've got doesn't buy us out,' Dougie Grant objected.

'I become a majority shareholder. I see myself as a sleeping partner. With my money and your knowledge of silver mining, production can be doubled. We work hard, review the situation in twelve months. By then anything could be possible.'

'I don't like it,' Swift said.

'That's because you're a lazy bastard,' Gallagher said scathingly. 'You've got your mind set on the good life in California, when the blunt truth is we've got no choice other than to accept Ablett's offer. Turn him down and within days we'll be forced to walk out of here with nothing. Accept, and this business could become a gold mine.'

Grant chuckled at the Scotsman's choice of words. Even Swift managed a weak smile.

Ablett tasted his drink, covertly admired the expensive cut glass, and kept quiet while the three directors left the table and went into a huddle on the other side of the room.

He gave them five minutes. Then he drained his glass, and deliberately put it down close to the swollen saddle-bag.

'My time is valuable,' he said clearly. 'The Silver Lode is the business I'm keen to buy into, but there are others. Originally from New York, my search has taken me from El Paso, through Nogales, and all the way to Yuma. I'm most impressed by your Tombstone enterprise, and by the opportunities in the San Pedro Hills — but I need a decision, now.'

He had their attention. They returned to the table. Swift looked at Ablett, and glanced briefly but pointedly at the saddle-bag.

'You say that in there there's exactly half of what we discussed?'

'To the dollar.'

Swift grimaced. 'All right. As you say, half is better than nothing at all.' He looked at his watching co-directors. 'It's a formality, I know, but let's have a show of hands.'

Gallagher's hand shot up. Grant

hesitated, then he too raised his hand.

'No need for mine,' Swift said, 'because two out of three means the motion's been carried. I guess that's it — welcome to the Silver Lode, Ablett.'

At once, the tension leaked out of the atmosphere. Fresh drinks were poured. Ablett tipped the money out of the saddle-bag, and the mood became celebratory. More drinks brought warmth into the conversation. Gallagher became interested in Ablett's business background, and the bank robber was happy to regale him with stories that were only partially true.

'You say you were recently in Nogales?' Gallagher said when the conversation stalled.

'There, then on through Sasabe to Yuma,' Ablett said.

'I was in Benson only yesterday. There's a telegraph there, as you know. News was in about a deputy marshal being shot dead in Sasabe — did you hear of that in your travels.'

'Yes, but it was the marshal who was

killed, not his deputy,' Ablett corrected. 'Bank robbers shot dead the town marshal, name of Hawker.'

'Well, if that's your understanding of the matter then I'm afraid you've been misinformed,' the Scotsman said. 'The report was quite detailed. Deputy Marshal Will Hawker was murdered — as you say, by bank robbers. His brother, Marshal Slade Hawker, raised a posse and set off in pursuit of the bank robbers. Unfortunately, there was bad news in a wire he sent from bank Yuma. The three members of the posse had been shot dead. Two bank robbers were also shot dead, but the leader made good his escape. Marshal Hawker was returning to Sasabe.'

Ablett was suddenly aware that the Scotsman was watching him closely as he told his tale. Swift and Grant had also stopped talking to listen, and now they seemed to be waiting for Ablett's response.

So numb with shock was Ablett's brain that it refused to send signals to his extremities. The fingers of both hands were locked around the whiskey glass.

He was unable to prise them loose. Carefully, he lowered hands and glass to the table. He looked up and managed an astonished smile. When he spoke, it needed an intense struggle to keep his voice steady.

'What a small world it is,' he said. 'I realize now I actually spoke briefly to that man in Yuma. He was wearing a badge, and he told me he was from Sasabe. I assumed he was the deputy, probably insulted him by addressing him as such. I really must take the time to make another trip to Sasabe and attempt to correct my mistake.'

*   *   *

'I believe it's time to move on,' Slade Hawker said.

It was a week after his return from Yuma. He was sitting at the table in the one big living-room in his house, eating a hot supper prepared for him by Mollie Creed. She was sitting across the table from him. Flushed from the heat of the stove, her auburn hair attractively in disarray, she was listening intently — without, Hawker noticed, any of the surprise he had expected.

'Do go on,' she said. 'If this is just a craving for excitement, then I'm all for it. But there's more to it than that — isn't there?'

'Oh yes,' Hawker said.

He ate a mouthful of beef steak, deliberately taking his time, marshalling his thoughts; wondering, he admitted, how much to tell her.

'All of it,' she said with a quirky little smile as she accurately read the indecision in his eyes. 'Hold nothing back, Slade.'

He sighed, pushed away his empty plate.

'Sounds ridiculous,' he said, 'but I was away from Sasabe too long. Or, let's say that while I was away, too much happened.'

'And what happened here in town was handled with such skill that it suggested to certain men with power that your services might no longer be required?'

'That's right. In a manhunt that took us most of the way across Arizona Territory and was plagued by ill luck and bad decisions, I let an outlaw and killer get clean away. Because I raised the posse, I'm deemed responsible for the death of three good men. The best I could come up with after a round trip of close on four hundred miles was that Manson's brother was murdered in the Yuma Pen. Here, the rustlers we've been hunting for a year were caught. Not by me, but by the young men I deputized before leaving.' He shook his head gloomily. 'County sheriff was more than impressed.'

'You've been Sasabe's marshal for just three months. For nine months before that, the ageing man who preceded you did no better.'

'But the young ones who came after

succeeded in seven days.'

'Still wouldn't be enough,' Mollie said perceptively, 'if you hadn't got another black mark against you.'

'Mm. I'm living with a married woman. Your husband, Alexander, has been throwing dirt and the ladies who attend church regularly want me — '

'Run out of town,' Mollie said softly. 'But if you run voluntarily, won't everybody be crowing?'

He grinned. 'If they are, we'll be too far away to hear.'

'How far?'

'Tombstone.'

'Can you get your old job back?'

'Earp promised to keep it open. For some reason he didn't think I'd last too long down here.'

'And he was right. But what about Nathan?'

'He's doing what he's good at, working with Charlie Birrel.'

'And living above the Buenos Tiempos.'

Hawker nodded. He could see

nothing wrong with the arrangement at the saloon. A woman would see it in a different light, but Mollie was sensible and while feeling responsible for her son she would also recognize that for Hawker there was no future in Sasabe.

'Putting distance between you and Alexander is no bad thing,' he said softly. 'And arriving in Tombstone with a ring on your finger and a man at your side — even if the ring's another man's — would be an — '

'An innocent deception?'

'A fresh start.'

She nodded. Her eyes were sparkling.

'I can see how it could be done,' she said, her eyes darting about the room as her thoughts raced.

'Charlie Birrel's got a buckboard he doesn't use. We could borrow that, and he and Nate would help us load up.' A small frown creased her smooth brow, and when she continued there was a warning in her voice. 'But if we are going to do it,' she said, 'we do it tomorrow, or not at all.'

'I'm so keen I was going to suggest we do it yesterday,' Slade Hawker said, straight-faced. 'We would have done, too, if only I'd had the guts to raise the subject sooner.'

PART TWO

THE RECKONING

11

Slade Hawker was standing at the bar in Tombstone's Eagle Brewery on the corner of Fifth and Allen Streets when Virgil Earp walked up beside him and put a hand on his shoulder.

'Old Man Clanton just rode in with his sons, Ike and Billy. The McLowrys have been in town all day, so keep your eyes open for trouble, your hand near your gun.'

'Sure,' Hawker said, and he watched as Earp, dark and powerful, with an impressive drooping moustache, moved away to make his presence known to card players and cowboys and the small groups of mine owners who were talking and drinking whiskey while managing to remain secretive about how they were making money from the silver-bearing ore discovered by prospector Ed Schieffelin in 1877 on the claim he named Tombstone.

It was late afternoon on Hawker's seventh day back in the job of Tombstone deputy marshal under city marshal Earp. Upon his and Mollie's arrival in Tombstone, Hawker had laid out some of his savings to buy a small abandoned cabin on the outskirts of town and with clear views of the Dragoon Mountains. It was dry and in good shape. Clearing up had taken a day, and they'd then unloaded Birrel's buckboard and turned the empty rooms into a home.

That morning he had left Mollie in the cabin clearing away the dishes after breakfast, and ridden into town for what had become a regular early meeting with Virgil Earp and his brother Wyatt, who was a Deputy US Marshal, shotgun messenger for Wells Fargo and a quarter owner of the Oriental Saloon and Gambling Hall.

Wyatt Earp had expressed his view that sooner or later all hell would break loose in Tombstone, and he'd named the Clantons, the McLowrys, Curly Bill Brocius and John Ringo as the outlaws sure to be in the thick of the action. In Hawker's opinion he should also have mentioned Doc Holliday, the murderous dentist, gambler and gunfighter who had spent time with Earp in Dodge City and who was an unpredictable killer. If Hawker was any judge, the explosion of violence that Wyatt Earp was expecting would certainly involve the outlaws he had named, but the match igniting it would in all probability be struck by the tubercular Holliday.

However, figuring that a gunfight that might take place at some time in the future was of no immediate concern, Hawker left Virgil Earp's formidable presence to keep the peace in the Eagle and stepped out into the cooling air. After a brief glance around he strolled along Allen Street and into Campbell & Hatch's Billiard Parlour where two men were involved in a game.

Hawker sat down to watch.

He was feeling pleased with himself.

The decision to move from Sasabe to Tombstone had been inspired, in seven short days he had seen Mollie Creed change from a nervous creature continually looking over her shoulder to a relaxed and confident woman who had already begun to make new friends; and as for his job as deputy marshal under Earp, well, he realized now that he should never have listened to Sheriff John Behan's advice and walked out.

The click of the billiard balls was strangely comforting yet, despite their lulling effect, Hawker was becoming aware that one of the players was glancing his way more than was normal, or polite. He waited, eyes half closed. A minute or so later the man sneaked a look in Hawker's direction for what must have been the fifth or sixth time. This time he realized that the deputy marshal had noticed his interest. He shook his head, laid his cue on the table and came over.

'Sorry if I appear rude,' he said, 'but I heard your name for the first time today. Seems we've got a mutual acquaintance — name of Zeke Ablett.'

He was a big man with a broad Scottish accent. The jacket of his dark suit had been shed to allow freedom of movement. His string tie had been loosened, and his white shirt was blotched with sweat.

'Yuma,' Hawker said at once. 'Three weeks ago, we got talking in a saloon, he gave me some news I didn't want to hear.'

The man grinned. 'He said something like that. Also mentioned he might have insulted you.'

Hawker was puzzled.

'When did he tell you this?'

'My name's Gallagher. I'm one of the directors of the Silver Lode Mining Company. We've been having a hard time. Ablett's a businessman from New York. He provided funds that saved our bacon.'

'Of course.' Hawker nodded, recalling the conversation in the Yuma saloon. 'I knew he was heading this way. We talked about how he should make the trip, Wells Fargo overland stage, or the railroad to Benson followed by a short ride south.'

'He took the stage. Pretty trail-worn when he arrived.'

'And now?'

'Well, like I say, the man believes he insulted you. I don't know the details, but the perceived indiscretion's disturbed him and I know he wants to make amends. He mentioned heading down to Sasabe, but now . . . '

'I'm here, he's here, so . . . '

'So you might as well ride up to the mine and introduce yourself. It'll give Zeke Ablett the opportunity to put right what he feels was a terrible mistake.'

★　★　★

Hawker was delayed somewhat the next morning. The meeting with Wyatt and Virgil Earp was spent discussing the Clantons and McLowrys. They'd left town after midnight, and Wyatt was now of the opinion that trouble in the near future was unlikely. However, he insisted that there was still the need for vigilance. In the past, Old Man Clanton and four of his men had been ambushed by Mexicans for rustling a herd of their steers. They'd been involved in the hold up of a Wells Fargo stage and, in clashes and near gunfights between the factions, Wyatt had pistol-whipped both Old Man Clanton and Tom McLowry.

'Trouble will come, and when it does it will be bloody,' he warned Hawker as the meeting broke up. 'Maybe this year, maybe next, but those embers are smouldering and when they burst into flame there'll be one hell of a showdown.'

And so, much later than he'd intended, Slade Hawker collected his horse from the livery barn and rode out of town. He rode towards hills shimmering in the heat haze, following directions given to him by the Scotsman, Gallagher. Less than an hour after setting out he was dismounting outside the offices of the Silver Lode Mining Company.

Gallagher came out as he was tethering his horse.

'Bad luck,' he called from the open doorway. 'Ablett left early this morning. Best I can offer you is some shade, and fresh coffee.'

Hawker confessed, as coffee was poured and he sat down at the long table with Gallagher and Doug Grant, another director, that he wasn't particularly disappointed at missing Ablett.

'He believes he insulted me, but I really don't know what he's talking about.'

'He reached that conclusion, and got pretty agitated, when I was telling everyone about some news I'd picked up from a Benson newspaper,' Gallagher said.

'About me?'

'Sure. Mentioned you by name: Marshal Slade Hawker, of Sasabe in Pima County. You'd sent a wire from

Yuma about a chase halfway across Arizona, a failed attempt to stop a killer making his escape by way of the Yuma Crossing. I mentioned some of this to Ablett. He said he'd spotted your badge when you met, but assumed you were a deputy.'

Hawker, nursing his coffee, frowned in disbelief.

'And that was an insult?'

'That's what he said.'

'Wouldn't be an insult,' Hawker said, 'unless he addressed me as such. Even then it would be a minor slip over which I certainly wouldn't take offence. As it happens, he never addressed me by any title, and I never told him my name.'

Doug Grant shrugged. 'Then it looks like this imagined slight won't be fully explained until Ablett returns — and from what he said he could be away for up to four days.'

The three men drank their coffee in a companionable silence, broken occasionally as one man made a remark about mining or Tombstone in general, and the others chipped in with their own experiences or predictions. Hawker briefly mentioned the trouble between the Earps and the Clantons. That evoked rolled eyes, and a consensus that blame should be shared equally, but that if it ever came to a showdown the Earps and Holliday with his hidden shotgun would defeat the outlaw faction.

'I'll try to stay out of it,' Hawker said, as he stood up and prepared to leave.

'You do that,' Gallagher said. 'In many ways it's a private feud that's been going on for some time. But innocent bystanders will inevitably get caught up in the crossfire so, yes, stay well clear and let them get on with it.'

Hawker, heading for the door, heard the Scotsman's advice and nodded vaguely, but his attention had been drawn to a couple of worn saddlebags hanging on a wooden hook. His eyes narrowed. Faint images stirred. The ghostly sound of racing horses, of distant gunfire crackling in the desert heat caused him to shiver. Memory began to stir as if from a restless sleep, and as words spoken or overheard struggled for his attention he recalled how a businessman in a dark suit reported seeing two men heading for Yuma Crossing, the older of the two carrying saddle-bags.

'These saddle-bags Ablett's?' he said, not turning, his hand reaching out to touch the dry leather.

'That's right. I guess when he rode out this morning he forgot them.'

Hawker felt numb. He swung to face the Scotsman.

'You say Ablett bought into the business. How were the funds provided?'

'In cash.'

'Which he brought here . . . ?'

Gallagher nodded towards the wall peg.

'In those bags — or one of them. Tipped it out on this table. Bundles of greenbacks.' His shrewd grey eyes were on Hawker. 'He told me later he carried those bags with him on the stage, then bought a horse in town and rode out here.'

'He carried them a hell of a sight further than that,' Hawker said bleakly.

Gallagher, elbows on the table, chin resting on his laced fingers, was nodding slowly. It was he who had read in the Benson newspaper details of Hawker's ill-fated manhunt with the doomed posse. Now his agile business mind was racing through a number of ugly possibilities. Doug Grant was also putting two and two together. His chair scraped as he rose from his seat. Grim-faced, he moved towards Hawker.

'A hell of a sight further, Marshal. Does that mean all the way from Sasabe to Yuma before he boarded the coach for Tombstone?'

'Almost certainly.'

'Then Ablett's bought into the Silver Lode using stolen money?'

'Yes. If we're right — if I'm right — Ablett's real name is Clyde Manson, and the money was stolen from the bank in Sasabe.'

'And this Manson, after following him for two hundred miles you stood next to him in Yuma, a glass of beer in your hand, while he told you the man you were chasing had taken the Yuma Crossing.'

Hawker grimaced. 'I'd arrested his younger brother for murder, but I'd never set eyes on Clyde Manson. The man I chased across the desert was an outlaw, a bank robber, a killer — he'd gunned down my brother. The man I spoke to in Yuma was wearing a dark suit and fancy boots and he talked of silver mines and speculators and how he needed to get to Tombstone in a hurry.'

'He played you for a sucker,' Gallagher said drily, 'but don't take it too hard because most honest men would have been fooled. He's a clever son of a bitch. Says he's from New York where he's been in business and, strange as it seems after what you've told us, I tend to believe him.'

'So where is he now?'

'Benson. Similar business story: there's a telegraph there, and he aims to find out if shares that hit bottom when he was in New York have recovered enough so he can recoup some of his losses.'

Hawker lifted the saddle-bags off the hook and slung them over his shoulder.

'The stolen money he brought here to buy a stake in your company has gone into the banking system' — he looked questioningly at Grant, who nodded — 'so with that off his hands he'll feel secure. However, I've been back in Tombstone for a full seven days. If Manson's got wind of my return, that trip to Benson may be pure fiction and he could by now be halfway to anywhere.'

'If he is,' Gallagher said, 'you've lost him again.'

'So all I can do is wait.'

'You want my gut feeling?' Gallagher said. 'Clyde Manson will be back. And when he gets here, Marshal, you'll be the first to know about it.'

12

The setting sun was turning the skies to the west into fiery splendour behind banks of misted purple hills when Clyde Manson eased his weight in the saddle, twisted this way and that to stretch stiffening joints and muscles, and looked contemplatively ahead to the sprawling town. Painted by the crimson light of the evening sun, shacks became fairy tale cabins, taller false-fronted buildings were transformed to become palaces erected from warm sandstone for gowned eastern potentates.

Yet as Manson drew closer the sinking sun began to cast longer shadows; with nature's paint stripped from them the true nature of the shabby buildings was revealed and, with painful nostalgia, Manson found himself comparing the uninspiring scene unfolding before him with the impressive structures he had turned his back on when he left the city of New York.

He had rented offices close to the New York Tribune Building, the highest on Manhattan Island. Several times he had used the hydraulic elevators in the Equitable Life Assurance Building — simply for their novelty, and to say that he, Clyde Manson, had been there. Yet none of the clear evidence of progress and wealth that surrounded him had saved him from bankruptcy. He had sunk like a stone into the murky waters of debt, had left with his reputation in tatters — and for what?

To see his brother sent to a stinking prison in the Arizona desert by a small-town marshal not fit to clean his boots. And in that prison, his brother Ben had died, murdered by a fellow convict.

The bitterest pill to swallow was that he, Clyde Manson, though several steps removed, had been ultimately responsible for his brother's death. Lured by reports of rich veins of silver buried in the hills surrounding Tombstone, Arizona, from his New York office he had done serious research that led him to the Silver Lode Mining Company. But there was a snag. The mine was not for sale, it was not looking for investors, and its owner, Frank Hainsworth, was a tower of strength it would be impossible to remove. Without hesitation, Manson had arranged for Ben to make his way to the booming Arizona town and there gun down Hainsworth.

That was when everything started going south.

Ben got drunk, did indeed gun down Frank Hainsworth, but got himself arrested.

Manson's business collapsed. He was left with no money to invest in the silver mine that was now there for the taking, and without money he was unable even to think of bribing the Yuma prison warden called Hogg he knew was corrupt.

But the fortune Manson had lost testified to his indomitable will, his refusal to be beaten.

A bank robbery in the Pima County town of Sasabe had provided him with all the money he needed. The town had been chosen because the alert marshal who had arrested Ben had since moved there from Tombstone. Convinced he was facing that lawman, Manson had stared coldly at him across a Winchester rifle's sights, pulled the trigger, and without realizing it had taken a brother for a brother. Some consolation, but not enough — and he had only himself to blame. If he had lingered for a few precious seconds when the lawman went down with a bullet in his chest, if he had screamed two names not one into the town's still air, or allowed the second man with a badge to come running up the street from the jail to face him, then the mistake might have been revealed and put right there and then. Instead, he had turned away to ride after Kemp and Guerrero, flushed with imagined success.

That imagined success had stayed

with him and led to another grave error: in Yuma he had let Hawker literally slip through his fingers because he believed the Sasabe marshal to be already dead, the man he was talking to a mere deputy. Again, he was a victim of his own stupidity. He had a tongue in his head yet once more he had failed to ask the right questions: in polite but pointless conversation he had done no more than discuss the relative merits of stage and railroad travel, and how he could best make the journey to Tombstone.

Yet, now, as he entered the town where the shadows of the street where splashed by pools of light from hanging oil lamps, Manson was able to brush away those gloomy thoughts as he would a light filming of trail dust. His brother was dead, half the money from the Sasabe bank had been taken by a corrupt prison warden, but he was now a major shareholder in a Tombstone silver mine. As a sleeping partner, he was able to leave the day to day running of that mine to the three directors. He had the freedom to put right his mistakes.

And so it was with a grim smile of satisfaction that Clyde Manson rode down Sasabe's main street and looked ahead to where the light was burning in the windows of the jail where he knew he would find, and this time kill, Marshal Slade Hawker.

★ ★ ★

'Stranger just come into town,' Nathan Creed said.

He'd been standing on the plank-walk outside the Buenos Tiempos saloon, taking the air. It was a warm, quiet night. A moon was trying to break through high, thin cloud. He'd watched Clyde Manson ride by, without any haste, and cut a diagonal path across the street in the general direction of the livery barn. Watched him swing down and lead his horse in through the wide doors.

Charlie Birrel was at the bar drinking neat whiskey when Creed walked back into the warm glow of the saloon where he had recently worked as a swamper and now lived in a sparsely furnished but clean upstairs room overlooking the street.

'Strangers arriving in Sasabe have generally lost their way,' Charlie said.

'Maybe he's one step ahead of a posse and about to cross the border.'

'If you stretch the bounds of possibility, he could even have come here with the intention of staying awhile.'

'Hah! If that's so, first light will show him his mistake and he'll move on,' Creed said, quietly enjoying the repartee. Waiting for Charlie's next comment, he picked up his beer and took a good long swallow.

'We stay here,' Charlie Birrel pointed out.

'Yeah, but we don't know any better.'

'Unlike your, er — now, what the hell do I call him?'

'Who?'

'You know who. The man who's acting like your stepfather, but ain't.'

'I call him Slade,' Creed said, 'because what he's doing with my ma is honourable, but dishonourable — if you see what I mean — and doesn't label him with a term in general use.'

'Oh, it does, only what it amounts to is an insult,' Charlie Birrel said, suddenly serious. 'Your pa's said it many times, shouted it from the rooftops, so to speak.'

'One day,' Creed said, staring into his beer, 'he'll shout the wrong words too loudly at the wrong man, and get himself plugged.'

'This conversation,' Charlie Birrel said, 'has taken a wrong turn.'

'Maybe, but if that did happen it'd solve a lot of problems.'

'You're not seriously telling me you'd be happy for Alexander to take a slug?'

'Hell, no, of course I wouldn't,' Creed said, and then he ruined the retraction by grinning. 'Goodness me,

Charlie, I really don't know what came over me.'

* * *

Manson took his breakfast at the only eating house in Sasabe, which just happened to be directly across the wide main street from the jail. He ate at his leisure, letting the time pass, letting the sleepy border town yawn and stretch and decide if today was a day that warranted a full awakening or if, as was usually the case for such settlements, it was a day for doing nothing much more than laze around in the intense heat and wait for nightfall.

The bank didn't see it that way. The building was a little higher up the street. By leaning forward at his table, Manson could just see its stone walls. It was the first business establishment to open, the heavy door swung wide by a tall man with a beard. Manson was unable to suppress a smile as he sipped his strong black coffee and recalled

177

Kemp and Guerrero tumbling out of the building with a sack of stolen money.

Then an uncontrollable frisson of anger caused the cup to quiver in his hands as he reminded himself that, while Kemp and Guerrero had been carrying out a classic, faultless bank robbery, the wrong man had been running towards the bank toting a shotgun; wearing a badge of office, running towards his death — about to die in his brother's place.

Well, today it was big brother's turn.

When Manson walked out of the eating house he took a few moments to stand in a relaxed way in the shade of the ramada — as any man might who has just eaten a heavy meal. But all the time his eyes were busy, for he knew that while the bank might be the first business to open, the jail office across the street had never closed.

Was Slade Hawker in there?

Only one way to find out.

But first, prepare for a fast getaway.

Manson walked down to the livery

barn and collected his horse. He handed a silver coin to the hostler. Then he swung into the saddle and rode the fifty yards back up the street and dismounted in front of the jail.

He tethered the horse using a loose hitch that would require a single jerk to pull free. Then he walked the few yards across the dust, hitched his gunbelt and stepped up onto the plank walk.

$$\star \quad \star \quad \star$$

From the window above his gunsmith's workshop, Charlie Birrel was watching Manson with a frown. He knew the man was a stranger, and assumed he was the rider Nathan Creed had watched enter town.

What bothered Birrel was that there was something about the stranger that was familiar — which made him less of a stranger than he'd first thought — but he was damned if he knew what it was that was setting warning bells jangling.

Couldn't be his face — from that

distance, the man's features were unclear. Couldn't be his clothing. Range clothing is nondescript at best, and in any case a man can dress differently from one day to the next.

So — what was it?

Rubbing his hand across his chin, feeling the rasp of whiskers, Birrel knew it was past the time for his morning shave and reluctantly moved away from the window. Time enough, he decided, to maybe look deeper into the background of intriguing strangers when he'd opened up shop for the day, when Nathan Creed had arrived and was at his bench working on his pa's damaged Colt revolver, and when the stranger himself had finished with his business at the jail — which, judging by the last glimpse he'd had of him, was where he was headed.

* * *

The man sitting with his feet up on the desk was a youngster. He was stocky, broad across the shoulders. Curly hair was so shiny it appeared wet. His gunbelt was on the desk alongside his boots and his Stetson. The belt with its filled shell-loops was wrapped around the holster, but, as he walked in from the bright sunlight, Manson noticed at once that the six-gun's butt was within easy reach of the deputy's right hand. Might be a struggle to get it out, could slow down his draw, but . . .

Where was Slade Hawker?

'I'm looking for the marshal,' Manson said.

The young man grinned and shook his head.

'No, sir, you're looking at the marshal.'

Manson glared. 'I don't know what that's supposed to mean, but I was told Sasabe's marshal was Slade Hawker. An older man. His brother was shot dead in a recent bank raid.'

'He was. And Slade Hawker was Sasabe's marshal. But after that bank raid and Will's death, things didn't work out for him. I'd been deputized for the time he was away hunting outlaws. In the end I was moved up a step. Sasabe's now got a Marshal Maguire, and Hawker's moved on.'

'To where?'

'Back where he came from. Tombstone.'

Manson rocked back on his heels. He masked his intense mortification by frowning and pursing his lips, when in truth he felt like kicking the young marshal's feet off the desk and stomping his head into the dirt floor. He could feel every nerve in his body quivering. A tick in one eye was causing his eyelid to jump. He rubbed it with a knuckle, shook his head as if in acute disappointment.

'When did Hawker leave?' he said curtly.

'More than a week ago.'

'Damn,' Manson said softly. 'I own a silver mine — in Tombstone. I could have saved myself a tiring trip.'

'Could that,' the marshal said affably. 'My advice is to rest up, then head for home.' He smiled apologetically. 'Could be boring, there's never a lot to occupy a man in Sasabe.'

'I'll find something,' Manson said.

When he stepped out onto the plank walk and looked up the street, his eyes were immediately drawn to the sunlight beating down on the stone walls of the bank.

★　★　★

'What's Alexander packing while you're fixing his Colt?'

'He's not. I guess he figures he's safe enough in the bank without a gun for a couple of days. What's that old saying? Lightning doesn't strike twice in the same place?'

Nathan was absorbed. He was sitting at the bench in the gunsmith's rear workshop, bent over the dismantled six-gun. The firing pin had snapped. He was ready to fit a replacement, but was taking his time because he was fascinated by the intricacies of the slickly oiled working parts of the fine handgun.

'The Chinese have another,' Birrel said. '*Fool me once, shame on you, fool me twice, shame on me.*'

'Yeah. Come up with one maxim and there's always another recommends the exact opposite,' Nathan said, without looking up.

Birrel chuckled, then strolled into the front shop and left him to his work.

It was almost ten o'clock and the sun was turning the dust of the street a dazzling white. Looking out of the window was almost too painful to bear, and Birrel walked over to it and reached up to pull down the blind. He paused, his hand on the cord.

'Well, well,' he said softly.

The stranger was there, outside the bank. He must have finished his business in the jail and ridden up the street. Now he was dismounting. Birrel watched him tie his horse to the rail — using a loose hitch, far as he could see — then walk a few paces back. He stopped there, turned, and for some reason stood looking down the street, apparently watching the jail.

'Goddammit,' Birrel said, feeling his scalp prickle as he stared at the man's back. 'Nathan, get out here, fast.'

There was a clatter in the back room, the scrape of a stool. As the stranger, apparently satisfied with what he'd seen, turned back to the bank, Creed came rushing into the shop. He joined Birrel at the window, his hand on the older man's shoulder.

'What's going on?'

'*That's* going on.'

Birrel pointed at the stranger, who had finished his observations and was now approaching the bank.

'Couple of seconds ago he was standing looking down the street. I saw a man in that self-same pose a couple of weeks ago. That fellow was holding a Winchester and watching Will Hawker advancing up the street towards him.'

'The bank robbery,' Nathan said. 'So?'

'Dammit,' Birrel said fiercely, 'I can't be sure, but unless my memory's playing tricks on me that fellow walking into your pa's bank is the same man I saw two weeks ago — the man who gunned down Will Hawker.'

He took a deep breath. When he turned from the window Nathan Creed was already running for the door.

* ★ *

Walking into the bank was like walking into a dusty schoolroom, Clyde Manson thought. Brought back memories of teachers wearing undertakers' suits, of iron discipline, and he wondered absently if that was the way the atmosphere had hit Kemp and Guerrero.

There were no customers. The tall man with the beard was coming around the counter. He wore a dark suit. The jacket's lines were unbroken by any unsightly bulge at the hip, and Manson knew he was unarmed. He went to a wall calendar to change the date, glanced only briefly at Manson. His eyes were hard, his face set and grim, and Manson knew instinctively that this man bullied his way through life along rigid straight lines he himself had laid. He would never bend. If money was to be taken from his bank, in his presence, it would need be taken the hard way.

A coldness descended over Manson. He slid his Colt from its holster, walked close to the big man. He lifted the six-gun, cocked it, and pointed it straight at the man's face.

'Twice in two weeks,' he said in a conversational tone. 'Goes on like this, you'll have no money left.'

'Beat it,' the man said.

'I guess folks usually listen to you — '

'I am Alexander Creed, I am manager of this bank — '

' — but not today, fellow — '

'Jakes!'

The man half turned his head to call the name. Then he simply looked at Manson and waited.

Stand-off.

Manson stood holding the pistol. Creed stared at him without blinking. Then there was a loud bang and a man burst through a door at the rear of the room, behind the counter. He was old and thin, but he was carrying a shotgun.

Creed heard the noise, knew exactly what it meant.

He lunged at Manson.

Manson shot him. The bullet drilled a black hole in the bridge of Creed's nose. The hard eyes went blank. Momentum carried him forward on folding legs. He slammed into Manson. Nerveless hands, clutching fingers, plucked at Manson's clothes. Then the bank manager, dead on his feet, slid to the floor.

As he went down, Manson dragged his legs free from the dead man's enfolding arms and leaped to one side. From beyond the counter the shotgun roared. Buckshot whistled through the air where Manson had been standing. It peppered the wall. Puffs of dust were drifting motes in the slanting rays of the sun.

Manson snapped two quick shots at the counter and, out of the corner of his eye as he turned to run, he saw the old man throw himself to the ground. Without waiting to see if the shots had hit home, Manson sprinted for the door. He dragged it open and leaped out onto the plank walk. Bright sunlight hit him in the face. Dazzled, disorientated, for an instant he stood there squinting left, then right. Then, the six-gun forgotten in his right hand, he leaped into the street and ran to his horse.

A man was running across the street towards him. He wore a black hat. Silver conchos glittered on the band. He was drawing a six-gun. Another man was emerging from a shop behind the advancing man. On iron brackets a gunsmith's sign creaked in the hot breeze. Down the street at the jail there was no sign that the shooting had been heard. Not yet.

Ice-cool now, Manson jerked his horse's reins free and swung easily into the saddle. The man running across the street — very young, Manson noticed — abruptly skidded to a halt in the dust and stood with legs apart and braced.

'Clyde Manson, stop right there and throw down your gun,' he yelled. 'You're wanted for the murder of Will Hawker — '

Manson used his left knee to bring his horse around. That put his left side towards the youngster. He was holding the reins in his left hand. Without making any sudden movement, he brought his right hand across his body and from under his left arm he shot the young man twice in the chest. He seemed to straighten. With a startled look on his face he took an unsteady step backwards, another. Then his legs buckled. The six-gun fell from his hand. He collapsed in a crumpled heap. As his head hit the ground, his black hat was dislodged. It rolled in a half circle, fell in the dust.

Still running, the grey-haired man who had charged out of the gunsmith's shop drew level with the downed youngster. He was medium height, but broad. Blue eyes were shining in a face weathered to old leather. He was dressed in shirt and pants. No weapon visible, Manson noticed. He'd heard shots and rushed blindly out of his shop, something he could live to regret.

Fractions of seconds crawled by, giving the impression that time was standing still. In those fleeting moments the gunsmith took one swift look at the young man lying face down in the dust. A six-gun lay close to the dead man's hand. It might have been the gunsmith's salvation — but he ignored it. Without breaking step he charged towards Manson. His arms pumped. His bare hands were clenched into fists. He was charging at a man on horseback holding a cocked six-gun. Manson couldn't believe his eyes.

What he *could* believe was the movement he detected at the jail. In a replay of the events of two weeks ago, a man wearing a badge was on the plank walk and looking up the street for the source of the commotion.

Time to move.

Without bothering to take aim, Manson fired a shot at the enraged man bearing down on him. The bullet hit home, off centre. The man spun, then sank to his knees with his mouth gaping in shock.

Manson's abiding memories of Sasabe would be of the gunsmith down in the dust and beating the hard muscle of his thigh repeatedly with his fist in his frustration, the young marshal standing in the street with a rifle to his shoulder.

He took a last look, heard the crack of the rifle, the whistle of the bullet flying close to his ear. Without thought, in a final moment of senseless bravado, he rode towards the two downed men, hung from the saddle like an Indian and scooped up the youngster's black hat. Then he wheeled his horse, raked it with his spurs and rode out of town.

13

Clyde Manson rode hard for an hour, pushing his horse without any real awareness of direction, intent only on putting Sasabe well behind him. He knew that very soon he must make a difficult decision, but his first concern was for his own freedom; without that, any decision would be wasted.

So, as the weight of the desert sun began relentlessly to slow the pace and the rivulets of salt sweat trickling down his face were dried into a stiff mask by the hot wind, he was patiently recalling his brief talk with Sasabe's young marshal. The conclusion swiftly reached was that from such a short meeting it was difficult to judge a man's character. Nevertheless, Manson was willing to bet that two men dead and another down wounded would have ruined the youngster's day — especially as the young marshal had watched the drama unfold. Question was, what would he do now? Western tradition said he'd raise a posse and go after the killer. But it was only a matter of weeks since Slade Hawker had tried that, and he'd been the only member of his posse to make it back to Sasabe alive.

That disaster would make the new marshal and those employing him think hard about a possible recurrence, and very likely hold back — an inevitable reaction, and one that would give Manson time to . . . to what?

With an hour gone, some twelve miles behind him and still no idea where he should go, he pulled off the trail and let his horse find its way into a dusty hollow where a trace of clear water seeped from an underground spring.

Manson dismounted, dropped to one knee to fill his water bottle, then left the horse at the spring with dipped head and trailing reins and sat on the slope in the shade of a scattering of mesquite bushes. The dead youngster's black, flat-crowned hat was on his head. His own Stetson hung from the saddle-horn.

As he sipped the ice-cold water, he couldn't escape the realization that he had reached another crossroads in his life.

Behind him there was a rich career in New York. Between learning of a silver mine in a booming Arizona town and his brother Ben being locked in the Yuma Penitentiary for the murder of the mine's owner, that career had blown up in his face. The decision to raise the money to buy his brother's freedom had been a good one, but a prison fight and a skilfully wielded knife meant that a bank robbery followed by a race across the Gila Desert had bought him nothing but his brother's body which now lay buried in the Yuma cemetery.

Yet, though his brother was dead, Manson had managed to buy a stake in the Silver Lode Mining Company. He was back in business, a major share-holder in an enterprise that was at the forefront of a rush to mine the precious silver ore.

Trouble was, that silver mine was in Tombstone — and so was Slade Hawker. Manson had once again gone on a killing spree in the town of Sasabe. Hawker would get wind of that, and come looking for him; would do so even without those latest killings, because Manson had gunned down his brother.

Manson leaned back against the tree, tipped his Stetson forward against the blinding sun.

There was no future for both of them in the same town. So, what to do?

The easy option was to point his horse towards the east, board the railroad at El Paso and enjoy the ride back to New York. He knew the financial markets, his absence would have dulled competitors' memories, in a short time he would recoup his fortune.

That was the easy option, Manson thought, watching his horse nibble at

196

the sparse green grass around the spring, but it was the one that was so unimaginable that it was impossible. No, the only option was to return to Tombstone, and avenge Ben's death. However, he had to do it in a way that left him free to continue as a director of the Silver Lode Mining Company.

Manson thought for several minutes. Then he threw back his head and laughed out loud. He had been going over conversations he'd had with his fellow directors. Dane Swift had talked at length about Virgil Earp's continuing trouble with a bunch of maverick outlaws. There was someone called Old Man Clanton, who was backed by his sons, Ike and Billy. Then there were the . . . McLowerys, McLowrys? . . . and a couple of villains, Johnny Ringo and Curly Bill Brocius.

Now, if he, Clyde Manson, couldn't use a few of the dollars he had lifted from the Sasabe bank to persuade one of those Tombstone desperadoes to pick a fight with Slade Hawker, or simply put a bullet in the deputy marshal's back one dark night — then he was a bad judge of men. Any one of them would do it for the money, without compunction, and would agree that the money that changed hands would also buy their silence.

Climbing to his feet with the conviction that he had found the answer he was looking for, Manson thought for a moment, then mentally clarified the condition he would put to the man he was going to pay to kill Slade Hawker.

When the deputy marshal went down, he, Clyde Manson, must be there to see it happen.

14

Thirty-six hours later

It was gone midnight. Slade Hawker, on duty as deputy marshal, was in Ned Doyle's recently opened Oriental saloon, the classiest drinking establishment in Tombstone. The carpeting was plush, and a pianist was playing a medley of melancholy tunes. On another night Hawker might have been listening to the sound of violins.

He had been circulating, keeping an eye out for trouble, and was now idly watching Wyatt Earp deal faro. It had been a long day, and it was becoming an even longer wait. Earlier, Hawker had spoken to Gallagher, who'd been in town most of that afternoon. The Silver Lode director had told him that when he left the mine, Zeke Ablett had not yet returned from Benson.

Quickly bored with the gambling, Hawker wandered over to the ornate bar and ordered a glass of beer. He was standing facing the doors when he was amazed to see Charlie Birrel walk in. The Sasabe gunsmith was travel-stained. His face was drawn, his head drooping with weariness, and there was an unsteadiness in his walk that Hawker knew was the result of too many hours in the saddle. He felt a ripple of apprehension when he noticed that the gunsmith's left arm was in a sling.

Inside the door, Birrel paused. His bright blue eyes swept the room, swiftly spotted Hawker. He grimaced, shook his head, and came over.

'I don't suppose this is about the buckboard,' Hawker said warily.

'In a way it is,' Birrel said. 'There's no easy way of saying this. Clyde Manson rode into Sasabe. While there, he gunned down Alexander Creed and Nathan. Both of 'em're dead. That's where the buckboard comes in: Nathan and his pa are already buried, but I'm willing to turn straight around and take Mollie back to Sasabe so she can pay her respects.'

Literally rocked back on his heels with shock, Hawker could only narrow his eyes and try to come to terms with the realization that Manson had once again done the unpredictable.

'He told his fellow directors he was going to Benson. What the hell was he doing in Sasabe?'

'Looking for — '

'Yeah, yeah, I know, he went there looking for me.' Angrily, Hawker slammed his fist backwards against the front of the bar. 'So once again I'm to blame for needless, mindless killings — '

'Cut it out. Manson talked to Maguire, the new marshal, and when he discovered you weren't there he decided to take a second stab at the bank. *That's* why Alexander and Nathan died, and that's how I got this.'

Birrel awkwardly lifted his arm, displaying the soiled white sling.

'So where is Manson now?'

'If he didn't find you in Sasabe, where d'you suppose he'd be?'

'Depends what Maguire told him.'

'He told him the truth. About what you'd done, where you'd gone.'

'So's Manson's back in Tombstone — or on his way?'

'I'd say so.'

'And you'd be right. With the money he stole from Sasabe, he's bought into a silver mine. He's not going to walk away from that.'

'Maybe not,' Birrel said, 'but financial considerations are always going to come second to his consuming hatred for you. When he does get back, he'll be in town for one reason only.'

Knowing the gunsmith was right, Hawker turned numbly back to the bar. He ordered beer for Birrel, watched the gunsmith drink deep to wash the dust from his throat and briefly close his eyes with pleasure. For the next few minutes they stood chatting in a desultory way. Even while talking,

Hawker was tormenting himself with a mental rehearsal of the way he would break the news to Mollie of the death of her husband and son. At the same time he was aware of Birrel's watchful blue eyes never straying too far away from the door leading to Allen Street.

'One thing that happened back in Sasabe did interest me,' Birrel said at last. He had not turned his head, and seemed to be musing aloud. 'I was in the main street, Manson had burst out of the bank, plugged Nathan dead with two clean shots and winged me in the shoulder. Then I thought I was seeing things. I'll be damned if that feller Manson didn't ride over and pick up Nathan's hat from where it had fallen in the dust. Then he rode off with it, holding it up like it was some damn war trophy.'

★　★　★

Manson wasted little time after he'd reached his decision, and he rode unnoticed into Tombstone some eight hours ahead of Charlie Birrel. The town was somnolent in the late-afternoon heat. Without seeing anyone he recognized — not surprising considering the short time he'd actually spent in Tombstone — he slipped into the livery barn and questioned the hostler about the whereabouts of Old Man Clanton.

'Newman Clanton,' the hostler said, spitting a stream of tobacco juice. 'That's his name, and that's what you call him if you want to stay alive.'

'I will, when I meet him,' Manson said, idly spinning a bright silver dollar.

Clanton and his sons, the hostler told him when he'd pocketed the money, had been ranching on the San Pedro river since 1877. He gave rough directions and, with dusk fast approaching, Manson set off in a south-westerly direction. He reached the Clanton ranch in less than an hour. By then it was full dark. When he had made himself known to men who didn't volunteer their names, Newman Clanton was summoned and he came out to talk to Manson on the ramada.

'I've a chore I want doing,' Manson said without preamble.

'What makes you think we're hired help?'

Clanton was a lean old man with a full grey beard. His ranch was obviously prosperous. Manson had heard vague rumours of outlaw activity and the rustling of Mexican cattle by the Clantons and the McLowrys, but Clanton seemed offended by Manson's bold statement.

'That's not exactly what I meant,' Manson said cautiously, feeling his way for the right tack. 'There's a man in Tombstone who was directly responsible for the death of my brother. That kind of wrong cannot go unpunished. I had the impression that you have men working for you, not necessarily Clantons, who could settle that score for me in a way that would be . . . fitting, and permanent.'

'You want him killed?'

'Yes.'

'His name?'

'Slade Hawker.'

'Ain't he Virgil Earp's deputy?'

'He is.'

Manson detected a change in Clanton's demeanour, and remembered the simmering feud between the Earps and the Clantons. It seemed he'd happened by chance on the right approach.

'My boys are too straight, they won't be interested and in any case I wouldn't condone that kind of criminal behaviour,' Clanton said. 'But you could go talk to Curly Bill. If he can't help you, there's a feller rode down here on a cattle drive with Curly Bill and Turkey Creek Johnson. Name's of Pony Diehl.' Clanton's grin was wolfish. 'Diehl's part Cherokee. What you're askin's likely to appeal to him — if the price is right.'

15

The next night a mood of extreme despondency hung over Slade Hawker. He was unable to shake it off.

After leaving the Oriental the night before he had taken Charlie Birrel back to his cabin and provided him with a makeshift bed. Then, unable himself to sleep, he had sat in a rickety chair on the small ramada gazing at the stars and left the gunsmith and Mollie undisturbed until sun up. Over a snatched breakfast, with the gunsmith there for moral support, he had held Mollie's hand and told her the bad news.

There had been no tears. They would come later, Hawker knew, but Mollie's one concern had been to set off as soon as possible on the long drive to Sasabe. She and Hawker had parted emotionally, but still dry eyed, and he had watched Birrel's buckboard rock and bounce down the street, Mollie sitting next to the gunsmith, straight-backed and stiff with grief.

Hawker had done very little for the rest of the morning. In the early afternoon he had ridden through the stifling heat to the ridge where the Silver Lode offices were located, stayed long enough for coffee with the three directors.

Swift, Gallagher and Grant were still trying to figure out what it meant in legal terms for them to be running a business on money stolen from a bank by one of their directors. Clearly, they'd decided, they were back where they had been before Manson — or Ablett, as they still thought of him — had appeared on the scene: sitting on a business short of capital and with no future. Hawker commiserated, but could offer no crumbs of comfort.

When he walked back out to his horse to ride back to town, there was still no news of Manson.

Hawker was not surprised. In Charlie

Birrel's opinion, Manson would be returning to Tombstone for one reason only: to exact his revenge on Slade Hawker. Hawker agreed, and knew that in the circumstances Manson would be a fool to show his face.

But where was he?

The question was still gnawing away at his subconscious when he arrived in town, stabled his horse, and ate a solitary meal in a nearby café. The rest of the day crawled by in aching loneliness. But when darkness came, the loneliness was pushed into the background by apprehension.

Hawker knew Manson would strike at night. Safety lay with bright lights and company. Wishing he had eyes in the back of his head, Hawker crossed the street and once again walked into the Oriental. He drank whiskey at the bar. He observed. He did his usual circulating to keep the rowdier customers in line. He saw no sign of Manson, and with the eerie feeling of being watched without knowing from which direction — or from which direction the fatal shot would come — he slipped into the despondency that became like a dark hole from which he found it impossible to escape.

The break came a little after midnight. Hawker was again at the bar, drinking more of the whiskey that was insidiously spreading numbness through his body and mind. The glass was at his lips when a man barged in from the street, looked about him, then saw Hawker.

'You're wanted out here, Deputy,' he called in a low voice that carried. Then, without waiting for a reply, he released the door he'd been holding open and was gone.

Carefully, Hawker put down his glass.

Nobody, it seemed, had noticed the man at the door. Faro was being played at the far end of the room. Wyatt Earp was watching. The pianist was playing the same melancholy tunes — probably the only ones he knew. Occasional bursts of laughter disturbed the gentle murmur of conversation.

What would it take to shock them, Hawker thought? A gunshot? The scream of a man mortally wounded?

Abruptly, aware that despondency was making him morbid, he pushed away from the bar and strode towards the door. As he walked, he checked his six-gun, eased it gently in its holster and was at once appalled by the lack of feeling or flexibility in his fingers.

When he stepped outside onto the plank walk, it was like walking from a Turkish bath into an oven. The heat, even after midnight, was enough to stifle a man's breathing, to cause his pulse to quicken in protest.

A man was standing in the centre of Allen Street. There was no moon. There were few oil lanterns, and those that were lit smoked badly. As Hawker waited for his eyes to adjust after the brighter lights of the Oriental, he thought that the man was exceptionally dark of complexion, possibly an Indian; and he was aware that well back in the shadows of buildings on either side of the street, other men watched and waited in silence.

The man in the centre of Allen Street called, 'Hawker?'

Hawker stepped down into the dust, moved out of the shadows.

'I'm Hawker. Who are you? What do you want?'

'It's not about what I want.'

'Did Clyde Manson send you?'

'Someone sent me. Someone paid me.'

'He wasted his money. I'll count to three. If you've not moved away by then, you'll spend the night in jail.'

The man chuckled.

'One,' Hawker said. 'Two — '

Still chuckling, head back and eyes shining, the man went for his gun.

Dulled by the whiskey, Hawker was almost caught cold. He saw the man's hand dip to his holster, yet the answering signal from Hawker's brain took too long to get started, and when it did it took too long to reach his hand.

He was fatally slow. Death was staring him in the face. Then his unknown adversary's six-gun snagged on the skirt of his loose jacket. He uttered a curse. There was a tearing sound as he ripped the weapon free. The six-gun came up. His thumb drew back the hammer.

Gunfights are won or lost by fractions of seconds. Coarse cloth had delayed a fast draw and given Hawker hope. Even his fumbling fingers and drink-dulled reflexes were fast enough, because the delay had been a very large fraction of a second and that was all it took to give him the winning advantage.

When Hawker fired, the other man's weapon was still rising. He took Hawker's slug in the centre of his body. His grunt was that of a man punched hard in the guts. He folded, stubbornly refused to go down; then he sank down on both knees, leaned forward on his hands, head hanging.

Hawker walked over to him. He kicked the man's weapon out of his hand, heard it slither under the plank walk. Then he lifted his foot, placed it on the man's shoulder, and gently pushed him sideways into the dust. The dying man's eyes were open, white and blinking. He shook his head. His teeth bared in a grotesque grin.

Behind Hawker, a man said softly, 'I always wondered what they meant by the luck of the draw.'

Startled, Hawker swung around. The voice had come from the shadows on the Oriental side of Allen Street. Once again Hawker's eyes were betraying him. He had adjusted from the saloon's brightness to the comparative gloom of the street, enough for him to find and hit a live target. Now he needed to adjust again for the shadows — and it was taking time.

But in those shadows, something glittered. Head high. Hat high. And as his scalp prickled, Hawker remembered Charlie Birrel's words.

I'll be damned, the gunsmith had said, *if that feller Manson didn't ride over and pick up Nathan's hat from where it had fallen in the dust.*

Hawker lifted his six-gun, cocked it, took a pace forward.

'Manson?'

'Who's Manson?'

'The man who murdered my brother. The man who rode into Sasabe a couple of days ago and murdered a bank manager and his son. The man who sent that' — Hawker jerked a thumb over his shoulder — 'after me because he hadn't the guts to do his own dirty work.'

'Ah, that Manson,' the man in the shadows said — but now the lightness and humour had gone out of his voice. 'So, what makes you think I'm Manson?'

'The hat you're wearing,' Hawker said, his eyes fully adjusted. 'I'd know that hat anywhere, feller — but I still can't see your face.' He lifted the six-gun, took a bead on the unseen face three inches beneath the glittering silver conchos.

'Step out of the shadows,' Hawker said. 'Do it now.'

The man took a step forward, then another. Then he stepped sideways. There was an oil lamp hanging from a bracket on the Oriental's wall. The light fell on his face.

The man was not Clyde Manson.

Hawker let his breath go explosively. He lowered the pistol.

'The hat. I told you I'd recognize it anywhere, and that's not changed. So, where did you get it?'

'I bought it. I saw it, liked it, the man wearing it was willing to sell.'

'What man?'

'I don't know his name — but he's standing behind you.'

★ ★ ★

The bullet hit Hawker in the back. The powerful blow knocked him flat on his face. Dirt was in his mouth. He could hear his own breath wheezing in his chest as the nerves in his body began to shut down. He rolled, blinked. Turned his head to spit dust. Gasped, his mouth hanging open. He realized he was looking up at the stars. The six-gun was still clutched in his hand. Dead man's grip he thought, irrationally. Laughter bubbled.

A second shot kicked dirt in his face. A third snapped the heel off one of his boots. His leg jerked. Instinctively he rolled again and came up on his knees. His back was warm and wet. There was no pain. He was breathing — but with difficulty. Breathing — and searching the shadows outside the Eagle Brewery on the other side of Allen Street with eyes that had created their own mist.

Out of the shadows and the mist stepped Clyde Manson.

'It's over, Hawker. My brother died by the knife, you die by the bullet. What do they call it? Retribution? An eye for an eye that is acceptable because it sees justice done?'

'Your brother went to prison for murder and was himself murdered,' Hawker said hoarsely. 'My brother was murdered — by you. Alexander Creed was murdered — by you. Nathan Creed was murdered — by you. And you certainly had a hand in the murder of Morg Stanley, Wes Costigan, Arn Mills . . . '

He broke off, panting. With a curious vibration beginning to course through his body, he sat back trembling on his heels. But the impact of the bullet striking his flesh seemed to have cleansed his body. Whiskey induced numbness had fled. His mind was clear; the mist was clearing from his eyes. He was aware that behind him the doors of the Oriental had been flung open. Light was flooding out. Men were crowding the doorway, the plank walk, watching and listening.

It was also clear to Hawker that Clyde Manson was hanging on to this moment. He had dreamed of revenge. His every waking hour since young Ben Manson had been locked up had been filled with images of Slade Hawker defeated, down on his knees, a broken man — and he couldn't let go.

That was a mistake.

Slade Hawker lowered his head. On his knees, he deliberately swayed sideways, recovered. Held himself upright — as if with difficulty. Let his breath rattle in his throat. It was as if a great silence had descended over that part of Tombstone. In the oppressive heat there was a funereal stillness. Yet that stillness quivered with tension. Something had to give. Something had to snap.

'End of the line, Hawker,' Clyde Manson said.

Once again, for one last time, he raised his pistol. But he was taking too long. Savouring the moment.

Hawker, down on his knees, bleeding, feeling that onset of sickness and light-headedness that comes from loss of blood, lifted his six-gun and fired a single shot.

In some eerie way, as Hawker watched Clyde Manson crumple, stagger back against the wall of the Eagle Brewery and fall heavily to the boards to lie there unmoving, it was as if that single shot he had fired became two detonations, two muzzle flashes.

Seeing double, hearing double, he thought — and that was his last thought before weakness overcame him and seeing, hearing and feeling all became lost in the enveloping darkness.

Epilogue

Slade Hawker was still in Allen Street, midway between the Oriental and the Eagle Brewery. On his back in the dust. His shirt had been torn open. The night air was warm on his skin as he gazed up at the stars. Then the stars were blocked from view as out of the shadowy circle of morbid onlookers a man bent over him, leaned close. A man with a dark, sweeping moustache, piercing eyes set in a lean face under slicked back dark hair.

Wyatt Earp.

The deputy US marshal's frock coat fell open as he leaned over Hawker. His shirt was a startling white in the gloom.

'You'll live,' he said. 'Bullet hit bone, got deflected and went straight on through. We'll get you to the doc. He'll strap you up, you'll be groggy for a couple of days; for a month you'll have trouble raising a glass, drawing a gun.'

'Is Manson dead?'

'And gone. Buckboard's been and moved his body, and Pony Diehl's.'

'That was the Indian's name?'

'Part Cherokee. Rode with the Clantons.'

'Manson,' Hawker said, frowning, trying to recollect. 'I fired once — but I heard two shots.'

'Yours and mine. You looked to be fading — '

'As I intended. I wanted him to think I was finished. Drop his guard.'

Earp nodded. 'Might have worked. I couldn't take that chance. I fired, you fired.'

'Who got him? You? Me? Or both of us?'

And now Earp was cagey.

'I didn't check. Manson's body's gone. If you want, if you feel strong enough to get to him before they plant him six feet under, you can look and see if there's one bullet hole or two.' Earp shook his head. 'If I was in your place, I'd leave it, because if the question remains open you'll have one hell of a story to tell your grandchildren.'

'Which is?'

'Can't you hear it, hear yourself talking to those youngsters sitting cross-legged in front of you?' Earp said, with the beginnings of a grin. '*When I was a young man,*' you'll say, '*back in Tombstone City's bad old days, I was involved in a gunfight with Deputy US Marshal Wyatt Earp — and, you know, to this day nobody can say for sure which one of us came out on top.*'

Author's Note

The outlaw, Pony Diehl did ride with the Clantons, but did not die in Tombstone's Allen Street at the hands of this book's fictitious hero! At the end of a short but infamous career on the wrong side of the law, Pony Diehl served time in prison, then simply disappeared.

We do hope that you have enjoyed reading this large print book.

Did you know that all of our titles are available for purchase?

We publish a wide range of high quality large print books including:
Romances, Mysteries, Classics
General Fiction
Non Fiction and Westerns

Special interest titles available in large print are:
The Little Oxford Dictionary
Music Book, Song Book
Hymn Book, Service Book

Also available from us courtesy of Oxford University Press:
Young Readers' Dictionary
(large print edition)
Young Readers' Thesaurus
(large print edition)

For further information or a free brochure, please contact us at:
Ulverscroft Large Print Books Ltd.,
The Green, Bradgate Road, Anstey,
Leicester, LE7 7FU, England.
Tel: (00 44) **0116 236 4325**
Fax: (00 44) **0116 234 0205**

SHOOT, RUN OR DIE!

Jake Douglas

Cody had once fought a cougar to a standstill — bare-handed. He's not a man to mess with. When Curtin and Willis rob him, leave his partner parboiled and burn down the cabin, there is nowhere for the killers to hide. Now a whole town want him for their sheriff — all but Deputy Blake Ross. He makes more trouble for Cody than he's ever seen, enough to plant him on Boot Hill with men he had hunted and killed.